My People

D1388327

In Memory of Professor Gwyn Jones

My People
Caradoc Evans

Introduced by
John Harris

SEREN

Seren is the book imprint of
Poetry Wales Press Ltd
Nolton Street, Bridgend, Wales

www.serenbooks.com
facebook.com/SerenBooks
witter: @SerenBooks

First published in 1915
This edition published in 1987
Reprinted 1992, 1997, 2003, 2014

ISBN 0-907476-81-3

A CIP record for this title is available from
the British Library.

The publisher works with the financial assistance
of the Welsh Books Council.

Published under the auspices of The University of Wales
Association for the Study of Welsh Writing in English.

Printed by the Grosvenor Group (Print Services) Ltd

Contents

List of Illustrations

INTRODUCTION: 'THE BANNED BURNED BOOK OF WAR'

Early in 1913 Caradoc Evans revived his literary ambitions and began to shape the material that soon would appear as *My People*. A thirty-six-year-old Fleet Street journalist, he had joined Edgar Wallace at *Ideas*, the popular penny weekly he in turn would come to edit. Journalism itself was a recent vocation: shortly after his fourteenth birthday Caradoc left school and his boyhood home, the south Cardiganshire village of Rhydlewis, to work as an apprentice draper in Carmarthen. This, he quickly discovered, was "the densest occupation in the world", and he bitterly resented the circumstances that had consigned him to it. Both his parents were of families of substance. On marriage in January 1870, his father William Evans (1849-82) settled at Pantycroi, a smallholding near to Llandysul on the Carmarthenshire border, although he aimed to become an auctioneer; William's bride, Mary (1848-1934), was one of the Powells of Blaenbarre, Rhydlewis, an influential land-owning family who somehow remained outsiders with a streak of irreverence within them. The Evanses were church people while the Powells were Nonconformists, like the bulk of farmers and cottagers. Though politics might deepen the divide, 'mixed' marriages were not especially frowned upon

9

provided that, as here, the families were socially matched. But this particular union outraged Mary's father, the more so after his son-in-law notoriously conducted the sale of a farm whose tenant had been evicted for defying, in the 1868 parliamentary election, the wishes of his Anglican-Tory landlord. Families thus dispossessed became martyrs to Liberal-Nonconformity and so great was public sympathy for them that local auctioneers withheld their services. Except young William Evans, recently qualified in that profession. The opprobrium long survived him, and as wife to such a man Mary Evans came to forfeit any share of her father's will, thereby condemning herself to poverty – for by 1882 she was a widow, her thirty-two-year-old husband having died of pneumonia. A mother of five – her fourth child, David Caradoc, was born at Pantycroi on New Year's Eve 1878 – she returned to her native village, there to struggle on the ten hillside acres of Lanlas Uchaf. As for Caradoc, his early experiences struck deep: "what we gather in our youth we commonly carry into our graves," he reflected. He saw his talents as thwarted for want of a proper education and became convinced that he would have proceeded to secondary school had help been forthcoming from his mother's brother, a highly successful medical doctor. But it was not, and the boy in consequence was put to drapery. Meanwhile Uncle Joshua gathered money and reputation: the two went hand in hand, material prosperity and public standing. "That is the way of the earth," wrote Evans at the time of *My People*; "If you struggle to put by a few pounds, you are called a miser. But put by thousands, and people will black your boots and whitewash your character."

For a decade or more he slaved behind shop counters, first in south Wales, then in London, the Mecca of all drapers. London was a liberation. Arriving there in 1899, he quickly took to the theatre and the music-hall, to pubs and late-night suppers, to browsing the second-hand bookstalls and tracking down literary landmarks, especially those relating to Dickens. In London grew the conviction that he was fitted for better things, and in hope of a change of career he embarked on evening classes at the Working Men's College, St Pancras. Two of his efforts in English composition actually appeared in print, encouragement enough for him to surrender his Bayswater berth at Whiteley's for a chancy opening in journalism. At twenty-seven Evans's mental horizons were expanding. Now something of a Christian socialist (if admiring of G.W. Foote, the vehemently anti-clerical secularist), he discovered books and reading, largely through *T.P.'s Weekly,* a popular literary paper "which exercised my brain and heated my imagination". He read Robert Blatchford's socialist *Clarion,* a journal marrying politics and literature, and the Sunday *Reynold's Newspaper,* badge of emancipated radicalism for Mr Doran in Joyce's *Dubliners* and the very first paper to publish Caradoc Evans. A dozen or so short sketches survive from these apprentice years (1904-07): mostly tales of the Cockney poor in the manner of Arthur Morrison and W.W. Jacobs, they were consciously means to an end; once fairly settled in Fleet Street Evans abandoned imaginative writing.

The return to fiction can be traced to conversations with Duncan Davies, the Lampeter-born draper's assistant whom Evans met first as a fellow employee at Whiteley's. A "very argumentative" union official opposing the loathed system of 'living-in', Davies became an important mentor, in politics and in literature. At the Evanses' East Sheen home – Caradoc had married Rose Sewell, daughter of a London job master, in 1907 – the two uprooted Welshmen swapped tales of home, material ripe enough, so it seemed, for fictional reworking. For years Evans had been storing local characters and incidents, many gathered on summer holidays at Rhydlewis. A nephew remembered him helping his neighbours with the haymaking: "With his coat off and his sleeves rolled up and a pitchfork in his hand, he would work all day, listening meanwhile to their conversation and watching for quaint phrases and ideas for short stories."[1] Other incidents had been with him from childhood, stories taken from his mother and the rebellious circle associated with Lanlas Uchaf.* An obituary of Mary Evans comments on her "wealth of reminiscences concerning the older residents", adding that "she also knew much of the earlier days of Nonconformity in Cardiganshire".[2]

Life was full of stories waiting to be written, or so Evans assured one London writing circle. Authors had to take their material from the people and events around them, then press the truth of their understanding, of their way of looking at things. "Thus the novelist should convince himself that his story is true before he begins to write it; in that manner he will be able to tell his story as if he were telling the truth."[3] As for choice of material, that was a matter of temperament and he made it clear where his own disposition lay:

> I like stories that are gloomy, morose and bitter ... An angry man is nearer himself than a happy man ... The Fury never leaves us; she abides with us for ever; she harshens the mellowness of our dying days. Love falls at the first stumbling block, and while she companied with us, we found her as insipid as milk and less interesting than a billiard ball.

The strength to abide by his vision, to harness "the Fury" creatively, Evans associated with his rediscovery of the Bible. It sharpened his sense of mission and gave him a stylistic model.

---

* "Many times have I sat with him in the kitchen of his mother's farm, near to Cardigan Bay, listening to her stories," the romantic novelist Edith Nepean remembered, and Evans attributed to his mother whatever gift for storytelling he possessed.

2. "Manteg in the quiet of Sabbath eve": Nanty, Rhydlewis

Bridge Street and Repair. Newcastle Emlyn.

3. "going over the bridge which spans Avon Teify she paused at the window of Jenkins Shop General"; Bridge Street, Newcastle Emlyn ("Castellybryn")

14

Having come upon the *Clarion*, it was Blatchford's "simple grandeur" that had led him to the English Bible. Now he picked up the Bible in Welsh, the very copy given him on leaving Rhydlewis as a boy. The Reverend J.J. Jones made the presentation, "a fat, impudent man, whose face was like the body of a hedgehog, but whose eyes had none of the hedgehog's gentleness. He scattered evil wheresoever he went, treading it into the earth with his heavy, flat feet." Detestation of Jones, and of his predecessor David Adams, had turned the boy against their book, but when now he began to read it the impact was dramatic. "I do not remember what made me take up a copy of it one Sunday night, nor what caused me to open it at the homely eighteenth chapter of Genesis [Abraham's intercession on behalf of Sodom]. I read that chapter seven times, and as I closed the Book I made a vow to write *My People*."

The younger Evans readily assumed the mantle of prophet and his words on Dennis Bradley (the West End tailor who brought 'Taffy' to the stage) as well applied to himself:

> Maybe he sat for years in his room near the sky, his eyes, like God's, on the street below; and the voice of God came to him, firing him with the command: "Tell the House of Israel of their sins, and the House of Jacob of their transgressions." This he does and with amazing courage and impudence – the courage and impudence that are conceived in belief.

Courage and impudence he did not lack, and the convictions that sustained them had grown immeasurably since he first approached his fictional world of Manteg. When once more his imagination drew him back to his native province, it was with a new understanding of his people's condition and how it had come about.

> I write down our condition to the tyranny of the preachers and the

> Liberal politicians. They have not only robbed us and given us a god of their own likeness – a god who imparts neither charity nor love – but they have dominated us for so many generations that they have fashioned our mind. They have built a wall about us. Within that wall – within the Nonconformist compound – we are born and spend our days in captivity. There are men who can break from any prison and our captors – our leaders – are the prison breakers.

Wales was in moral darkness because of religious tyranny. The challenge was to embody artistically this dreadful truth.

"I remember him referring to the language difficulty. To write in ordinary English would destroy the effect. Caradoc pondered over this matter for two or three weeks and evolved the idea of a basis of Old Testament diction, and afterwards he handed me 'the rat story'."[4] Duncan Davies calls attention to the stylistic roots of *My People*. The biblical cadence lends the narrative an air of authoritative proclamation, simple, often majestic, suggestive of myth or parable. Yet the Old Testament prose has another function, becoming a satiric weapon for attacking those who would commandeer biblical style and precept for their own personal gain. Ministers and deacons made the Bible their 'hateful weapon': Evans turns it devastatingly against them, impersonating what he would oppose. His Welsh-English dialogue is a unique creation, a compound of translation from the Welsh, aggressive mistranslation, and distorted English syntax. The mistranslations caused lasting offence – "white shirts" for *gynau gwynion* (not "white robes" or "heavenly raiments"), "Big Man" or "Great Male" for *Gŵr Mawr* or *Bod Mawr* (not the "Great Being" or "Almighty God") – but, argued Evans, "In the rendering of the idiom you must create atmosphere. If the Bible or Tolstoy were done into straight English none of us would get nearer the life and conditions with which these authors deal." Through dialogue he reveals the consciousness, the innermost feelings, of his characters; as they speak, so they are, no external analysis is necessary. A friend of his later years, the Aberystwyth academic George Green, has Caradoc say:

> I knew very well what *Bod Mawr* means in the dictionary or to a Welsh scholar. But I know very well what it means to the man I am writing about. He is quite incapable of thinking of a great being. A white robe means to him his Sunday shirt, complete with celluloid collar. I am trying to represent that man's mind and how it works. If he does not really say "Big Man", he thinks it, and his imagination will go no farther. It is what he ought to say if he were telling the truth about his thoughts, which is what I am trying to do.[5]

On the question of literary models, the Welsh-language playwright D.T. Davies recalled how Evans told him that during the writing of *My People* he had confined his reading to the five books of Moses and would have nothing to do with any word that was not in Dr. Johnson's Dictionary. The focus was narrow, but not that narrow. He ranked *The Pilgrim's Progress* next to the Bible ("the only two books that will help one to write – especially to write fiction"), and Bunyan would have provided an effective instance of biblical prose married to a racy vernacular. Like Evans, Bunyan shares the puritan's inclination to see the world in black and white, and favours a satire investing allegorical figures with dramatic and psychological interest. Applauding Bunyan's style, Evans found it "clear and simple and vivid", and so indeed is his own. We know that during this period he was also reading the continental realists (Maupassant, Zola, Chekhov, Tolstoy), the Victorian social commentators (Dickens and Gissing especially – to the end a portrait of Dickens would hang above his writing desk), and the playwright J.M. Synge whose work, so Evans's Fleet Street colleague Austin Clarke insisted,[6] inspired *My People* (Synge's disciplined anger and bold refashioning of language to convey a cultural reality makes him a plausible model). Outside literature, Evans credited the music-hall artist Marie Lloyd as having influenced his narrative approach. She let her audience fill in the blanks; or, as he put it, "She tells a story not by what she says but by what she does not."

The fifteen stories of *My People,* many cast as highly concentrated life histories culminating in a dramatic situation, are all variously interrelated, the strength of the collection deriving from a tight geographical framework and further linking devices of character, action and theme; from what strikes us, overall, as a coherent social statement. "My People" are "the peasantry of West Wales" (as the subtitle elaborates), more particularly, Evans's kinsmen and neighbours, the inhabitants of his fictional Manteg. Rhydlewis is the village, "in the parish of Troedfawr" (Troedyraur), fixed by consistent references to Aberystwyth, Cardigan, Carmarthen and "Castellybryn" (Newcastle Emlyn). Rhydlewis sits in the vale of the Ceri, a river joining the Teifi westward of Newcastle Emlyn on its way to Cardigan town and the sea. At Rhydlewis the valley is a sweep of meadowland, bounded by high moorland to the east and south, while north and westward are gentler cultivated hills. "Manteg" is thus locked away in its shallow bowl: this would have been Caradoc's perspective as he toiled up and down the hillside between school and his childhood home. Lanlas stands on an eastward rise; the desolate moorland above it, scarred by quarry and gravel pit, he explored as a boy (the moor is a presence in *My People*). Local topography underpins his stories – names of local farms heavily influenced his fictional choices – and Evans took pains to get his detail right.

Besides specific locations, *My People* alludes to events, customs and beliefs peculiar to the locality: *Dydd Iau Mawr* ("Big Thursday", the village seaside outing on the second Thursday in August); fairs and other mileposts of the farming year;

4. "the First Men who occupied the high places": ministers and deacons, Four Crosses Chapel, Caernarvonshire

courtship rituals (stories regularly concern the getting of a wife); the figure of go-between and marriage factotum (Job of the Stallion in 'A Heifer Without Blemish'); the unscrupulous itinerant book-canvasser (Evans's "Seller of Bibles"); and the various superstitions associated with approaching death. As handled by Evans, they make for an unflattering view of the community, and in broaching incendiary issues (money worship, social hypocrisy, endemic brutality, the particular abuse of women) in a similar matter-of-fact way he inevitably provoked a backlash – how could he simply be reporting the facts? The question of the veracity of *My People,* of the literal truth of key incidents, is a minefield. A little local research will reveal the model for Nanni or Sadrach Danyrefail, and the *Western Mail* came some way into the open in 1924, remarking "Near Rhydlewis there lived a farmer and his wife. Mr Caradoc Evans calls the man Sadrach. His wife became insane, and she had to be locked in a room in the house, as was natural. That is all …" The horrifying details of Achsah's confinement we take as imaginative projection, yet even here there is some basis in fact: hospital records from late nineteenth-century Cardiganshire document a treatment of persons judged insane comparable with that afforded Sadrach's wife.[7] Evidence of this kind is interesting, though it does not crucially affect the success of 'A Father in Sion'; we accommodate the treatment of Achsah to our total sense of the story.

Evans displayed the practitioner's reluctance to discourse on method. He spoke of himself as a reformer, using the approach of a neutral photographer, apportioning neither praise nor blame. The nearest we get to a literary defence came in 1924 when, nine years after having insisted on the factual truth of *My People,* he challenged his newspaper critics,

Where have I said that my work was about Rhydlewis? Where have I said that my tale about the old woman and the rats is true? I do not

know a person, or act, or deed, or incident that will give me enough
matter to make a story … Why find fault because I write in the most
engaging way I know? Is the builder blamed because he builds well?

This declaration holds all the theory he thought necessary to
explain his fiction. His stories are more than the specific
characters or incidents they describe; instinct compelled him to
write in the way he did, and it was pointless to wish that he had
written otherwise; his stories are internally structured, coherent
and self-authenticating – "well-built", in his own idiom.

If Evans saw religious tyranny at the core of a monolithic
culture, he did not confine his fiction to the chapel and its
corruptions. *My People* has a social dimension not always fully
recognised. Ministers feature less directly than one might
imagine, being aloof, detached presences often working
through subaltern henchmen and often, so one senses, in the
power of these deacons (plate 4, the minister and diaconate of
a North Wales chapel, perfectly captures these elements). In
five stories only is the presence of a minister crucial; in two
they are barely mentioned, and in eight they are absent
altogether, even as passive bystanders. Repeatedly Evans calls
his ministers rulers or judges, and their resonant, hyphenated
surnames mark their social superiority. Dress too distinguishes
them (frock-coats, kid gloves, varnished walking sticks) and
their manner befits the enormous prestige Welsh society
conferred upon them. In 'Lamentations' Bern-Davydd, himself
a mouthpiece for God, addresses the village through gossipy
Bertha Daviss. His familiarity with the Almighty, so awesome
to his flock, invariably amuses Caradoc; whatever their wish for
deification, these men are all-too-human, their origins deeply of
the people, their domestic trials much as their neighbours'.
Wives can be difficult ("Come into the cowshed, sinners bach,"
Bryn-Bevan invites a chapel deputation, "the mistress has been
washing the flags"), and offspring a cause of anxiety. Bern-

5. "Chapel Sion": Hawen Chapel, Rhydlewis

Davydd family problems occupy 'The Redeemer'. At the age of
fifty-two, the inadequate Lamech prepares to follow his father
into the ministry, while younger son Adam, "imbued with little
understanding", languishes in Shop Pugh Tailor, threatening to
sink irredeemably by "going low for a female". A minister's
son, whatever his prospects and however strong the family's
need of an heir, must not stoop to "a workhouse brat".

'The Talent Thou Gavest' considers the making of a Sion
minister: his call to the pulpit, his period of doubt and
alienation, his subsequent reintegration into the faith and the
community. Eben, child of a widowed mother impoverished by
the chapel, initially thrives, possessed of those qualities making
for pulpit success: an easy emotionalism, a professed concern
for the next world (in face of the iniquities of this), and a more
than nodding acquaintance with the Almighty. Evans invests
his ministers with "singing eloquence", the capacity to beguile
by empty words and shows of feeling. Assayed by spiritual
misgivings, Eben abandons chapel magniloquence for the
everyday prose of social concern; he must preach "the real
religion" against the hypocrisy and injustice around him. The
new approach wins no applause, indeed is judged atheistical.
Evans knew the response at first hand, Nonconformity
holding, in the main, that socialism would lead to atheism, and
chapel leaders instinctively fearing the consequences of a rapid
social and political change.[8] The Roberts Shop Grocer incident
likewise reflects a harsh reality. A servant girl, sexually exploited
by a social superior, stood no chance in a court of law: she
would be dismissed as a scheming temptress ("Poor Roberts
bach was sorely tempted, and he is forgiven. And has he not
sent the bad bitch about her business?").[9] Money suppresses
conscience, as Ben Shop Draper understands. So Eben makes
peace with the community. "I have found the true light", he
announces – the light that blinds.

The notion of Welsh classlessness, assiduously fostered by Liberal-Nonconformity, barely survives a glance at south Cardiganshire at the turn of the century.[10] In an exclusively agricultural environment, size of holding is paramount. Farms of a hundred acres were considerable places and their occupants persons of standing; with a hundred and fifty acres a farmer would do a minimum of manual work, his time being taken up by farm management and marketing. As little as thirty-five acres could mean virtual self-sufficiency, but of the 203 occupied houses in Troedyraur parish in 1901, no fewer than 157 had less than thirty acres, with widows often looking after the very smallest holdings (Caradoc's mother, we remember, worked a mere ten). All these 157 households were in some measure dependent on the forty-six others. Work debts bound cottagers to farmers and in this finely graded hierarchy farmers of substance naturally enjoyed the highest social ranking. War only increased their dominance.* Evans sought accuracy in his description of farms. The accounts of acreage, the inventories of animals, are not there for rural colour: they sharply define an individual's social position. Sadrach farms Danyrefail "with its stock of good cattle and a hundred acres"; Silas Penlon has "nearly one hundred acres" and "ten cows and ten pigs and three horses"; at the beginning of 'Lamentations', Evan Rhiw possesses "fifty acres of land, a horse, three cows, and swine and hens", while at the end "he had ten milching cows and five horses, and he hired a manservant and a maidservant, and he rented twenty-five acres of land over and beyond the land that was his …"

Cottagers are likewise ranked, by land possessed and style of

* Outside his fiction, Evans railed against Welsh farmers, who were widely felt to be profiteering during the war, paying starvation wages, manning the military tribunals to keep their sons at home, and threatening with military service farm labourers brave enough to fight for better conditions.

dwelling. Simon and Beca ('The Way of the Earth') subsist on ten marginal acres above Penrhos, "their peat-thatched cottage under the edge of the moor", while Madlen ('The Glory that was Sion's') brings to Twm "two pigs, a cow and a heifer, several heads of poultry, and Tybach, the stone-walled cottage that is beyond the School-house". The cottagers suffer double exploitation, being inferiors both of the farmers and of the tradesmen and professionals in the community. The shopkeepers and local teacher constitute a small petit-bourgeois presence, often identified with the farmers and minister but not totally accepted by them. They are largely figures of fun, the tradesmen grasping for every ounce of profit and "that old blockhead" Lloyd Schoolin a lightweight among chapel elders and ineffectual in his job. 'The Way of the Earth' movingly delineates the exploitation of the weakest as the bankrupt shopkeeper, William Jenkins, schemes for the savings of Simon and Beca. The elderly couple live their lives by the only rules they know. "Shop General, Castellybryn" is "a godly man and one of substance", and they pray that this substance will be settled upon their daughter. Inevitably they are outwitted, and there is true pathos in the old man's pleading at the moment of defeat:

> Simon shivered. He was parting with his life. It was his life and Beca's life. She had made it, turning over the heather, and wringing it penny by penny from the stubborn earth. He, too, had helped her. He had served his neighbours, and thieved from them. He wept.
>
> "He asks too much," he cried. "Too much."

"He had served his neighbours, and thieved from them." The author's gaze is steady; he knows these purblind creatures, moving from birth to death across a remorseless landscape. As Beca understands, the way of the earth is not mysteriously determined; "it is the way of mortal flesh".

Worldly success and godliness are for Manteg one and the same. Material prosperity is a sign of God's favour: the Calvinistic message is writ across the land: "a godly man and one of substance"; "the strongest farmer in the parish of Troedfawr, and the saintliest man in the Big Seat in Capel Sion"; "Behold now, this man Evan is among the wisest in the Capel. And there's rich he is." Wealthy farmers were chosen as deacons, occupants of the Big Seat (*Sedd Fawr*) in front of the pulpit, and officers who, with the minister, comprised the governing body of the chapel. (The *Seiat* – Evans's "soul-searching assembly" – signifies a wider fellowship, the regular group meeting designed to bolster the faith of members, to admonish backsliders, and occasionally to expel them.) If farmers were elected deacons, tradesmen and senior craftsmen might be appointed teachers in the Sunday school or singing class. Smallholders and cottagers, however dutiful their membership and exemplary their lives, could rarely aspire to office. The same was true of women, of whatever rank: "Apart from Sunday school work and 'young people's' activities, the contribution of women was virtually limited to reciting a few verses when asked to do so."[11] With a chapel hierarchy so exactly reflecting the stratification of the everyday world, it is not surprising that social position should be equated with spiritual worth. Religion cemented the community, religious teaching and moral vocabulary being appropriated to sanction the manner in which society organised itself.

Manteg has its rebels. In 'A Just Man in Sodom' a harmless simpleton with leanings towards the pulpit becomes a disordered would-be prophet exiled on the moor. Pedr functions as some kind of social critic, castigating the adulterous ways of Sion and its thieving from widow and orphan. Yet he cannot make sense of the corruption save in terms of his community's religious primitivism. The Manteg dispossessed offer further seats of resistance, and in Twm Tybach ('The Glory that was Sion's') Evans allows a humble cottager one rare victory. The reprobate Twm frustrates the chapel, whose concern is with a show of strength against the heathen Church – with how many it can claim as its own, no matter their quality of faith. The story stands apart in other respects, drawing in incident and tone on the apprentice piece 'Taffy at Home' (1908) and preserving touches of "fine writing" that Evans came to abjure. Matters had decidedly changed by the time of 'Lamentations' and the persons of "the light men", the wild boys of the inn who humiliate Evan Rhiw by draping him in a mantle of skin stripped from a buried horse, having previously carried him into a stable and "laid him in a manger". The words of Luke, juxtaposed with what strike as elements of pre-Christian ritual, hint at unbiddable forces abroad.* "The light men" bring to mind that chasm in Welsh society between the godly and the worldly. The elect remain apart, shunning worldly pleasure, and with alcohol a critical touchstone, the polarization centres ultimately on the presence of a public house.† In south Wales Evans for the first time encountered a muted religious scepticism and there could claim

---

* Two localised horse rituals are seemingly here conflated: the Mari Lwyd, in which a horse's skull was used to frighten beholders – the ceremony is associated with Christmas and New Year revelry – and y ceffyl pren ("the wooden horse"), a form of public humiliation most often inflicted on individuals suspected of sexual misdemeanour. Significantly, it was a punishment Evans's own father had endured; local memory recalls him being carried on a wooden pole across the parish boundary north of Rhydlewis.

† Rhydlewis lost its own, the Gwernant Arms, after a sustained campaign for its closure led by the local Calvinistic Methodist minister. The Cardigan and Tivy-Side Advertiser could hardly contain itself: "The dreams of the inhabitants of the Rhydlewis valley have now been realised, and this place is now clear from an inn, as the sign of the Gwernant Arms has been taken down." (8 January 1915.)

the pub as a centre of social debate. That was never the case in the north and west, where (as he saw it) Nonconformity so pervaded the culture that dissent took the form, not of rational argument, but of a religious emotionalism yet more diseased. Memorably Evans fixes the inmates of his rural compound, prisoners and jailors alike: "As they were born; so will they live. They are victims of a base religion. They have been whipped into something more destructive than unbelief."

Story after story find men and women brutally opposed, for Manteg is a patriarchal society where men walk with God and women are deep wells of sin. The ideal wife is a servant, as Joshua explains ('The Woman who Sowed Iniquity'): "But then Priscila is content to stand where the little Big King has placed her – an angel ministering to me and my children." Her role is divinely sanctioned, a matter of some satisfaction in an agricultural community where the labouring capacity of a female guarantees a productive farm. It is a point rammed home by Deio to his wavering son Tomos ('A Heifer Without Blemish'): "You need a woman to look after the land, and the cattle, and your milk man. And after you." The young man sets out for the April fair in search of "a tidy female"; soon after ten in the morning the match with Nell has been made, leaving the rest of the day for pursuit of a heifer. The apportioning of time seems just: cattle deserve more attention than wives. Evans's stories often revolve around the search for a suitable partner, and in the attendant manoeuvrings women play their part, marriage being their surest means of social advancement. The consequences are usually dire – murder, madness, abandonment – though Martha succeeds, the "stranger woman" who comes to rule at Danyrefail ('A Father in Sion'). Sadrach's "gift from the Big Man" supplants the older wife Achsah; if men want women as workhorses, they also want them sexually; but as sex is evil, so must women be. Sex is always illicit, a male succumbing to temptation; when men fall, they counsel secrecy, which makes sex a weapon for women to achieve their goal.

My People stresses the reduction of women to servant if not animal status; they are beings owned and controlled, subordinate always to men. 'A Bundle of Life' shows male egotism as destructive of family feeling and ultimately of the man himself. Silas Penlon rightly senses in son-in-law Abram, "the chief singing man in Capel Sion", a challenge to his position as dominant male. Their social ranking is nicely conveyed: Silas's contempt for "a man of nothing" and his "foolish singing class" sits easily with a farmer of substance. Both are active Sionites, and Abram's recognition of the biblical quotation by which Silas drives his slave-wife Nansi affords a brief harmony between them. Then Abram starts to issue Nansi's orders: a "new King" is emerging. For the older man a collapse of identity follows, since masculine standing is crucial to public reputation and personal self-esteem. Abram's succession demands the complete abasement of his father-in-law, while the casting-out of his wife's first child (fathered by another) lays bare a primitive male rivalry. "Take you this brat of sin with you now, little people … for he is not of my bowels."

Hannah and Matilda ('Lamentations'), Shan ('The Blast of God') and the servant girl Lissi ('The Redeemer') are all defenceless women variously abused. Incest between Evan Rhiw and his daughter Matilda lies at the heart of 'Lamentations', although the matter is barely mentioned, as if the narrator's reticence mirrors the community's. Following his encounter with "the light men", Evan returns to a troubled Matilda, who meets his bizarre appearance with her own puzzling words: "Jesus bach, if the sons of men wear the habit of horses the daughters of God must go naked." The reference is to Genesis 6,2 ("the sons of God saw the daughters of men that they were fair"), a passage treating of an unnatural sexual union that must incur divine reprobation. In 'Lamentations', justice is stood on its head: Evan, a chapel elder, receives absolution on account of his offerings to the minister; "the adder" Matilda, abused to breaking point, is roped and led away to the madhouse.

Not all *My People*'s women function as the mute oppressed. We have the spirited, rebellious younger ones, like Sara Jane, a working girl emboldened by her looks ('The Way of the Earth'), and Esther, in 'Greater than Love' (a Caradoc Evans day at the seaside): they are dangerous forces in Sion, the greatest challenges to the way men see themselves and thus to be obliterated. Betti ('The Woman who Sowed Iniquity') suffers two-pronged abuse, from husband and brother. She is finally beaten down – "the Lord will administer the rod of correction on this slut" – though not before she has mounted some formidable resistance. A tangle of public piety and steely self-interest, Joshua stands with Sadrach Danyrefail as an archetypal man of Sion. Both are word-obsessed – Gwylim, savage husband of Betti, is also a "talkist" – a characteristic amusingly pointed in the contrast between the Almighty's matey parlance ("Well-well, Josh bach, very terrible is this about the wench Betti") and Joshua's own grave pomposities:

> Joshua leaned his body against the dresser, and drew his clog from his right foot and removed the dirt that had gathered on the sole between the iron rims; and he closed his mouth so that the projecting birth-tooth in the middle of it clawed his lower lip.
> "The Big Man brought my feet here, Betti fach," he remarked at last.

Here physical repugnance mirrors ugliness of character, while the dirt on Joshua's clogs reminds Betti that for all his god-like assumptions her brother's feet are of clay. In Dinah we encounter *My People*'s most immediately impressive female (one can only ponder Martha, the shadowy "stranger woman who rules at Danyrefail") and her story, 'The Devil in Eden', in which Manteg outwits a fallen angel, demonstrates the lure of the folktale for Evans from the outset of his career (it is all-pervasive in his final phase). The piece pivots on Dinah's responses to Michael, her knowing directness contrasting with her father's responses, all mediated through biblical quotation. Michael too quotes the Book, but this man is more than his words. "Dinah rested her elbows on her stockinged knees, and she settled her eyes on the sleeping stranger – a muscular figure with tanned, hairy skin showing under his buttonless shirt." She has her designs on Michael, who knows the ways of women. Dinah is Caradoc's New Woman – intelligent, watchful, sexually alive, and firm in the faith – the kind who in the later fiction increasingly gain the victory.

Yet the images that haunt are those of victimised women in stories of mythic dimension: above all, Nanni as suffering Wales, duped by a Bible salesman, sacrificing herself in her rat-infested cottage. 'Be This Her Memorial' is justly the most celebrated piece in the entire Evans canon, closely followed by 'A Father in Sion'. They were the earliest stories to be published (in the prestigious *English Review*) and one can hardly conceive of a more brilliant first showing by an unknown author than these 'Two Welsh Studies' of April 1915. 'Be This Her Memorial' considers a woman at the bottom of the heap. Nanni survives in her "mud-walled, straw-thatched cottage" on a weekly 3/9d in poor relief (the sum is mentioned three times), for which she is obliged to labour, and from which a tithe must be given towards "the treasury of the chapel". She is immune to circumstances, socially unawakened, representative of a far-back primitivism in the community. "Nanni was religious; and she was old … she was so old that her age had ceased to concern." Her age conditions her religion, and 'Be

This Her Memorial' explores the nature of her belief. The widow's life of sacrifice typifies the lot of the Manteg have-nots – the cottages of the poor are all houses of sacrifice – but Nanni's supreme sacrifice takes on a different dimension. Its potency disturbs Sadrach Danyrefail and the minister Bryn-Bevan, to the ultimate threatening of their rule. Her story might sound beyond time and place, to the eternal shame of those who made her condition possible. She needs a memorial and Evans will be her bard. Thus the "this" of the story's title is both Nanni's sacrifice and the story which forever proclaims it. Matthew 26,13 also comes to mind. "Verily I say unto you, wheresoever this gospel shall be preached in the whole world, there shall also this, that this woman hath done, be told for a memorial of her." The woman of Bethany anointed Jesus, recognising him as Messiah; Bryn-Bevan is Nanni's Messiah: "in her search for God she fell down and worshipped at the feet of a god". Never again would Evans break authorial cover in the way he does for Nanni. His practice is not to comment openly on the action, whatever the provocation, but to communicate through a deep, pervasive irony. (Opinion enough flows from his Sionite narrator, whose understanding – in summary, "the Lord comforts his children" – is always part of the story.)

'A Father in Sion' stands at the opening of the collection. The choice is wholly appropriate, for the story of Sadrach Danyrefail crystallizes *My People*'s preoccupations and best conveys this author's imaginative universe. With its blend of intensity and control, a narrative detachment yet admitting of genuine pathos and drama, 'A Father in Sion' is quintessential Caradoc Evans, down to its brilliantly arresting ending, one which shocks and reverberates, inviting various interpretations. In focusing upon a deacon and farmer, Evans explores the relationship within Manteg of religion and the social order. For

Sadrach religion is a matter of reading and mechanical obedience to the externals of the faith. Language has become, not an instrument for honest expression, but a means of forcing others. He cunningly appropriates the moral vocabulary of his community ("Christian", "respectable", "disgrace", "mad") and manipulates it to suppress and control. The women are his dramatic counters. Whereas he lacks in sympathy and free emotional response, his wife and daughter reach out to nurture and engage; his malign rhetoric and forcing of opinion contrasts with their seeing and knowing. Patterns of imagery underscore these distinctions: in particular, eyes and light are associated with the seers Rachel and Achsah. (The death of Rachel concentrates language and imagery most effectively. She dies "in the twilight". Moonlight for Achsah, twilight for Rachel: when wife and daughter succumb to a creature of darkness, it is appropriately in conditions of half-light.) 'A Father in Sion' stands as a most powerful and subtle indictment of the violation of individual conscience and feeling in a theocratic community. Sadrach represents a social and cultural omnipotence: "Of all who worshipped in Sion none was stronger than the male of Danyrefail; none more respected." The chapel is the cementing institution, furnishing an exploitable rhetoric and mythology. In Liberalism Evans detected the political arm of the chapel (the chapel "guides us to the polling booth where we record our votes as the preacher has commanded us") and in attempts to suppress his book he saw that arm at work.

The publishing history of *My People* begins with the two *English Review* stories of April 1915. Caradoc's delight at their appearance in the leading literary journal of the day was tinged with a certain anxiety: he knew his pieces were explosive and he seriously considered publishing them under a *nom-de-plume* that

These stories of the Welsh peasantry, by one of themselves, are not meat for babes. The justification for the author's realistic pictures of peasant life, as he knows it, is the obvious sincerity of his aim, which is to portray that he may make ashamed. A well-known man of letters and critic has expressed the opinion that "My People" is "the best literature that has, so far, come out of Wales."

6. Dust-jacket of *My People,* first edition (Andrew Melrose, 1915)

had served him ten years previously. With two more offerings in the next *Review* (July 1915), an Evans book-collection might have seemed a fair commercial proposition, although publishing wisdom held that short stories had no market appeal. Nevertheless, by November *My People* had appeared under the imprint of Andrew Melrose Ltd, a minor publishing house possibly recommended to Evans by the poet W.H. Davies who had recently signed to the firm. Whatever the initial contact, Melrose well recalled his first encounter with Evans. "When on a memorable day nine years ago, the author of *My People* came to see me, and I asked him if Welsh life and character contained nothing more beautiful than was revealed in that startling and mordant collection of sketches, he replied 'Oh yes, but it is the ugly side of Welsh peasant life that I know most about.'" Between them, publisher and author devised a marketing strategy that would have far-reaching consequences. A Scottish Presbyterian with a background in the Sunday School League, Melrose found the stories discomforting, but he understood their positioning in relation to Allen Raine, the romantic novelist whose idylls of Cardiganshire life had sold in prodigious numbers. Here was an answer to Raine from a writer of power and sincerity, much as Melrose's close friend George Douglas Brown had blasted the tender pieties of Scottish Kailyard writing with *The House With Green Shutters* (1901). "If you get sincerity and style you get literature at its best," wrote Melrose in relation to *My People*. Even so, he realised that the collection would seriously offend and among his conditions for publishing it was that it be given a "carefully worded jacket". The Melrose dust-jacket is indeed remarkable. Author and title statements are totally banished from the front cover, to be replaced by seventy boldly displayed words of introduction (see opposite).

Indicative of content, intention and worth, these sentences

had no small impact in England and were the only part of the book most Welsh reviewers thought it necessary to read. The title, too, was loaded: besides fixing a subject matter, it underlined the claim to authenticity. This was an insider reporting, "a Welsh-speaking Welshman, cradled in Welsh Nonconformity", as Caradoc described himself. The jacket's insistence on the stories as disturbing social documents jolted English reviewers and predictably inflamed the Welsh. The emphasis suited Evans. He considered himself a realist in as much as he faced grim fact, and he insisted on the truth of his writing, both its deeper assumptions and most of its surface detail. Yet fully to express his vision he freely moved beyond documentary realism, into scalding fantasy and black comedy of the grotesque. As for the opinion of the "well-known man of letters",* that the book was the best literature that had come out of Wales, this was seen in Wales as crass English ignorance, marked by an English wish to welcome anything that was patently anti-Welsh.

Published in early November, *My People* became for the *Globe* "easily the literary sensation of the moment". Evans spoke of "more than ninety reviews" and some forty can be readily traced. Overwhelmingly favourable, they ensured commercial success, three reprints being called for in as many months (December 1915–February 1916). The *Evening Standard* hailed "a strong, notable book"; "each story ... a triumph of art" (*Bystander*); "the power of the thing is altogether undeniable. For page after page Mr Evans holds you, as the Ancient Mariner held the Wedding Guest" (*Punch*). The stories were praised for their formal mastery ("not a single comment

---

* Thought to be Norman Douglas, the English Review's assistant editor who had helped bring Evans's work to prominence; "Douglas liked people of character, people whose idiosyncrasies had not been worn away to polished surfaces," remarks his biographer Mark Holloway.

or superfluous word mars their tense directness") and their
hauntingly personal style. Caradoc Evans was *sui generis* ("we
know of nothing to put beside these merciless, sardonic
silhouettes") though comparisons were evoked, with Gorky,
Zola and Maupassant and the English moral satirists. The *Daily
Herald* thought *My People* "the most poignant satire since Swift",
yet even Swift had penned no work "so cold, so detached and
uncondemning, so void of praise and blame". Here in truth
was Evans's hallmark: a calm dispassion, a freedom from
extraneous moralizing, the suppression of all emotional and
moral rhetoric. "He draws a picture of the life he has known –
to his own unforgettable horror and disgust – and the
incredible, the inescapable impression one has is that it is
largely true."

Inevitably, reviewers speculated on the factual basis of the
book – the *Globe*, for one, believed it had "no small
ethnological value" – or took up the question of "literary
realism". For Norman Douglas, Evans was a realist using non-
realistic techniques. "The book stands apart," he suggested in
the *English Review,*

> Realism has an eye for detail; pokes its nose into this and that;
> luxuriates. What Mr Evans tells us in his archaic language is too stark
> and austere to be realistic. He does not gloat or pry. He conveys,
> rather, a sense of elemental things – the coldness, the indifference of
> rocks and waters. He moves above his subject.

"Realism is an artistic method," expounded John Middleton
Murry in the *Daily News;* Caradoc Evans hated passionately, and
had "the power to control his hatred by an artistic method".
His stories showed a "splendid sureness" and "not one of
them offends, because beneath them all is the convincing
passion of the thing deeply felt or keenly seen. One never has
a tremor of apprehension concerning the writer's vision, or any

suspicion that he himself has evoked the ugliness which he portrays." This said, Murry foresaw the storm about to break in Wales and indeed got a taste of it when one Welsh reader complained that his newspaper praise was a greater crime than the book itself. Murry avoided combat: his praise was not to be taken as an endorsement of Evans's views of the Welsh; he had spoken of the peasantry of the book, not the peasantry of West Wales – and, "To admit that Mr Evans's view is inspired by hatred is to announce that it is one-sided." By and large the highbrow critics favoured literary readings, ones which universalised Evans's appeal; his was a world of the imagination where puritan vices were lashed in a prose strangely beautiful. Understandably, such detachment was impossible in Wales where attention firmly focussed on the book's non-literary dimensions. It was as the author intended. "If I had not made a *mwstwr* [commotion] in Wales I should have failed in the object I had in view – that of breaking down the power of Welsh Liberal Nonconformity."

Welsh reaction to *My People* was unremittingly, incandescently, hostile. No book before or since has remotely provoked such hatred. The onslaught began in April 1915: just two short stories from a newcomer (no more than 5,000 words in all), yet they sparked editorial reaction in five Welsh newspapers. With the appearance of *My People,* the *Western Mail* joined battle, denouncing a "squalid, repellent" collection, "false and miserably misleading". Conceived as a national newspaper by its editor William Davies, the *Mail* was striving to foster a sense of Welshness amongst a readership increasingly divided and exposed to Anglicisation; any attack on Welsh Wales was insupportable. So Davies thundered editorially against Caradoc – while granting him the right of reply (a facility gladly accepted). The *Mail*'s review is temperate compared with some other Welsh responses. The level of abuse still startles, directed at Evans's writings ("the literature of the sewer", "a farrago of filth and debased verbal coinage", "every page … teems with clotted idiocies"), his ugly face and dirty mind, his grasping, treacherous disposition – he was simply a writer on the make, feeding gobbets to the English "who love to live on filth". Evans remained composed; in fact he grew in confidence, convinced he had found his target. The gales of wrath amounted to little – something that did not surprise him. "If one speaks against us we denude the hedges for sticks with which to beat him. We stand before our accusers not with the rapier of reason or the shield of belief but with foolish phrases on our lips and mud pies in our hand." And indeed none of Evans's critics attempted any serious exposition of Welsh Nonconformist achievements. The instinct was to cling to their belief in a Welsh country heaven, spared the loss of language and religion, the class strife and social evil, that marred the industrial south. The Church kept Wales in darkness, so Evans was reminded, and Nonconformist blood had to be shed to let in the light. That these freedom fighters, the ministers, farmers, lawyers and tradesmen who drove the squire from the land, should in turn have oppressed the peasantry was a nonsense: victims cannot victimise. On the contrary, through its democratic chapel-based culture Wales had gained more than its share of the great – great preachers, great poets, great politicians – from all walks of life.

Evans was prepared to concede that life in the industrial south might be more democratic but,

> the head of the peasant chapel is the man of the pulpit, whose power, supported by the Nonconformist body, is as strong as that of the Biblical judges of Israel. He may not be a strong man himself, but he is strong in the sense that he has the impregnable wall of his religious organisation at the back of him. In such circumstances a weak man becomes a cowardly-strong man. Generations of his kind

have subdued the people over whom he rules: a people who believe the voice of God has called him to rule over them. He lives in the best house of the land of his chapel, he possesses more riches than any of his congregation, he makes opinion and destroys illusions …

The peasantry had been drained of substance through their attachment to Nonconformity – "a body which breaks down beliefs and traditions and all lovely things, and builds in their places hard materialism and avarice and hatred". There was no Wales to speak of, no real national life, for Nonconformity was the enemy of the imagination, repressive of art and literature, of freedom and independence of thought, of human feeling and the true welfare of the people. The country languished in self-ignorance, nursing its "sorry illusions"; and "Wales will never find a new national life until she sees herself as she is. It is my purpose to hold the mirror up to my countrymen, and by displaying their weaknesses, do something to stimulate the great revitalisation for which all patriotic Welshmen are looking." And a new Wales was stirring. Men were breaking free of their tethering cords, foremostly in the politically radicalised industrial south. "We are not dead," Evans would assure a Bangor student audience in 1924:

We have intellect. It is in the coal-pits, in the universities, and in the fields. The signs are clear that we are awakening. We have a group of writers and a group of politicians who are marching along; they are not faint of heart; they are marching with dignity and majesty and with great purpose. They and those who will come after them will create a new Wales or a Wales for the Welsh.

Such positive sentiment he rarely expressed; continuous attack was his chosen defence, a hacking away at the psycho-emotional roots of the Welsh establishment. Confident of national support, that establishment branded him a traitor, for to attack institutionalised Nonconformity was to attack the nation, and at the very time when thousands of his patriotic countrymen were dying on the Western Front. His was the dissident's knotty position, and in speaking to the outside world he committed the dissident's further crime.

Carrying one of the few uncomplimentary English reviews, the *Birmingham Post* recognised that the author's anti-chapel bias was "palpably political". This, of course, is true, and his book was politically persecuted. Attempts to suppress *My People* began soon after publication. Of the four great subscription libraries, Boots and W.H. Smith preferred to exclude it from their lists altogether, while the Times and Mudie's stocked it, but for restricted circulation only. They had got cold feet following the prosecution of Lawrence's *The Rainbow* on grounds of obscenity and shied away from handling another controversial title. Their stance encouraged action in Wales. On 10 January 1916 the Cardiff police raided Wyman's bookshop threatening to seize all copies of the book. The grounds for this action remain obscure: press reports talk of the police operating on a warrant in connection with the 1857 Obscene Publications Act, though a successful prosecution under this act must have seemed unlikely. Evans immediately suggested that David Williams, Chief Constable of Cardiff, was moving on the promptings of others; before Christmas he had read *My People* uncomplainingly but now had changed his mind, claiming, "I was for twenty years at Scotland Yard, and I read most of the suppressed books, and *My People* is the worst book I've ever read." Politics lay behind the volte-face. "In attacking Welsh Nonconformity you attack Welsh Liberalism," Caradoc averred; "they are one and the same thing. Every chapel in Wales has its committee-room in the interests of Welsh politics." Cardiff booksellers had simply been cowed into not stocking *My People*.

Against this unofficial censorship Evans determined to

fight ("Mr Williams may take it from me that he will not suppress my voice in a hurry"). He would bring the matter to court and, if necessary, to the House of Lords, "to prove that the police have neither the powers nor the rights to instruct the people as to what they should read." The matter was raised in Parliament* and a case against the police put into the hands of the solicitors. "I am prepared to stand my trial. I am prepared to say that there is no obscene phrase or suggestion in my book. But I am not prepared to be accused, tried, and convicted by a Cardiff policeman, whose actions are protected by his position." The Society of Authors rallied to his side, as did prominent literary figures: H.G. Wells thought *My People* "very finely done ... I am bound to do what I can in support of you" (though privately he confided that Galsworthy, Gosse or Barrie might be better witnesses than the author of *Ann Veronica*). However, since the police had seized no copies of *My People*, court action against them was well-nigh impossible. Meanwhile the charge of obscenity had been eagerly accepted in Wales, the *Welsh Outlook* (March 1916) declaring, "Its apparent lack of pornographic intent has succeeded in getting printed things that have never been printed before, except in the literature of deliberate pornography." The charge is ridiculous and gives credence to Caradoc's view that Welsh Liberals were moving against him, and at the highest level – for behind police intimidation he saw Lloyd George's hand. To others besides his compatriots Lloyd George epitomised the strengths of Welsh village Nonconformity, and such a

---

* By Colonel Arthur Lynch, Nationalist MP for West Clare, who appealed to the Welsh love of liberty and free speech "without which they would not have won the great victory of the disestablishment of the Welsh Church". There was more truth in Evans's peasantry than in "the comic-opera type tossing hay in silk stockings for West End audiences"; he was "a man of genius and a true artist" who "paints what he sees".

devastating exposure of the faith could only tell against the Minister of Munitions. Thus his sharp dismissal of Evans: "Pride of race now belongs to the lowest savage. This man is a renegade."

"We take leave to say that there is not a Welshman living of any literary note who will commend the narrative, and not a critic of standing who will dare sign his name to an approving estimate of *My People*." The *Western Mail's* lordly pronouncement proved to be largely true, though there were approving words from the political opponents of Liberalism. The socialist *Labour Voice* (previously *Llais Llafur*) hailed a new force in Welsh letters. Evans "can observe; he can write; he will be realistic though the heavens fall; and he has a sympathy as cordial as his touch is sure". *My People* was "by a long way the best book that any Welshman of our day has written". (Allen Raine, whose name others reverently evoked as the true chronicler of rural Wales, is dismissed for her "mushy sentimentality".) The reviewer was W.H. Stevenson, an ex-miner educated at Ruskin College, prominent in Labour politics. Formerly a journalist with the *Llais Llafur,* Stevenson had joined the *Daily Herald,* national organ of the labour movement, and might well have been behind the editorial that the *Herald* ran on the attempted ban on *My People.* It asserted Evans's complete sincerity. "For first and last – and let this be remembered of him and his work – he is a Welshman who passionately loves his people, and passionately hates the horror and hypocrisy of the evil things in their midst." Such a response was far from representative of the Welsh labour movement at large. Evans polarised positions, as at Cwmavon where older chapel men urged the banning of the book from the Tinplaters' Institute library; the younger men held altogether different views of "Comrade Caradoc Evans", or so the Merthyr *Pioneer* reported. Old-style Mabonite Lib-Labism sought a moderate, reformist programme, one which harnessed Welshness and religion; as when the socialist novelist Joseph Keating lambasted Evans in a *Western Mail* panegyric on his Valleys people, which linked their shining virtues – their radicalism, respect for art and education, their love of family, community and place – to their passionate devotion to religion ("Wales is a garden of chapels"). (It took a maverick of the Right to revitalise the belief that all that is best derives from family and community bound to a rural landscape, our childhood Eden and heart of the nation: "How green was my Valley, then, and the Valley of them that have gone.")

In Wales Anglican Tories proved altogether more admiring of the book – they spoke across a religious and political divide – and their west Wales mouthpiece, the *Carmarthen Journal,* offered unequivocal praise (uniquely for a Welsh publication, it tried to print some Evans fiction). The *Journal* published his defence of the stories in the *English Review,* a letter wryly alluding to the Christian charity of his critics: whatever their differing positions, they were agreed that "in a nicely conducted community I would, a handkerchief drawn over my eyes, have been placed against a blank wall long ago". His stories were fiction – "so far as I know, none of the incidents I have related has ever happened" – but no less real for that since they embodied truths about a particular phase of Welsh life. "My quarrel is not with religion," his letter of 23 April 1915 proceeds,

it is with the promoters of what is known as Nonconformity, a strong, powerful body who recognises no law except that of its own making, who has substituted God for the black-coated figures that oppress the people and drain them of their substance, who has succeeded in fashioning a large majority of Welsh peasants into creatures without stamina and without soul. This has gone on for generations … A pillar has been raised between them and Him and

the engraving on that pillar is 'Nonconformity'. What do you expect
from such a people? You get immorality and hatred and avarice …
You know all this is to be true, and you know of incidents more
remorselessly true than anything I have written about in my stories.

Nonconformity, the *Journal* agreed, had become a repressive
creed, a religion of feeling and sensation, and it translated a
piece from the Welsh-language quarterly *Y Geninen* practically
admitting as much: "Extreme sectarianism inevitably produces
a bigoted, revengeful and wholly unchristian spirit. One of the
direct effects of the sectarian spirit … is the lamentable rivalry
in erecting chapels where they are not needed … These chapels
are built on borrowed money, and the resources and energies of
members are strained to meet these financial liabilities, leaving
no room or means for real Christian work." The chapelgoer is
led to believe that so long as he contributes to the various funds
the exercise of faith can be neglected. "How can a working
man, with a weekly wage of, say 24/-, support a wife and family
and meet the endless demands for contributions?"

The *Geninen* article underlined from an inward
Nonconformist position much of Caradoc's thinking, and
distinctly enforces the view that for many in Wales his crime lay
not so much in what he said as in his choice of English for
saying it. The Reverend David Adams himself (one of *My
People*'s targets) had fulminated against the shortcomings of
Welsh Nonconformity, though he did so in a Welsh academic
journal, not in English-language newspapers or a book with a
London imprint. To parade Welsh failings before a gloating
English readership was misguided and unforgivable. A
Carmarthen Journal reader graphically makes this point when he
speaks of Evans's stories as providing ammunition for the
arrogant Englishman who "over his pint of beer in his squalid,
dingy gin-shops treats his neighbours with a lengthy
dissertation upon the barbarians who live somewhere on the

other side of the Severn". "Does he desire the utmost contempt of his countrymen? Does he desire his name to be handed down as a byword for treason? It is easily done ..." The questions were uncannily prescient. For the vast bulk of his compatriots the author of *My People* had alienated himself completely (their hatred, as he predicted, pursued him beyond the grave). Evans remained unmoved, writing shortly before his death of a "certain religious clique in Wales" for whom "the supernatural is everything and human charity nothing". They preach "temptashoons":

> not a word about farmers' wives who work three times harder than their husbands and for no wage. Not a word about dogs shut in an outhouse from Saturday night till Monday morning without a drink. Not a word about pale weak children who are denied the fruits of the earth by money-grubbing parents.

Grounded in local experience and fuelled by a deep personal outrage, *My People* is universal in its appeal and concerns. It treats of the evils of the world – the greed, lust and hypocrisy, the ineradicable conflict and injustice – in a manner wholly original and compelling. In Caradoc Evans' imagination and feeling are all the more potent for being under the tightest artistic control. Within a week of the book's publication, the *Evening Standard* proclaimed what would become a critical commonplace, that *My People* was utterly unlike anything previously offered from Wales. It was Evans's literary audacity, his work of liberation, his determination to survive artistically in the face of puerile abuse and abysmal misunderstanding, that won the admiration of a generation of writers in Wales for whom *My People* became the founding text of a new 'Anglo-Welsh' literature. The movement could not have wished for a more impressive beginning.

INTRODUCTION

NOTES

1 Howell Evans, letter to Marguerite Evans, 6 February 1945. National Library of Wales, Aberystwyth (NLW), Professor Gwyn Jones Papers.

2 *Cardigan and Tivy-side Advertiser,* 27 July 1934, p. 6.

3 From 'Advice to Young Authors', *Writer*, April 1925; reprinted in *Fury Never Leaves Us: A Miscellany of Caradoc Evans,* ed. John Harris (1985), pp. 131-6. This anthology includes Evans's autobiographical pieces and a selection of his polemical journalism, sources for many of the quotations used in this present introduction.

4 Duncan Davies, letter to Marguerite Evans, February 1945. NLW, Professor Gwyn Jones Papers.

5 Introduction to Caradoc Evans, *The Earth Gives All and Takes All* (1946), p. xxvii.

6 'The Bitter Word', *Irish Times,* 29 March 1947 (a review of Caradoc Evans, *The Earth Gives All and Takes All,* and Oliver Sandys, *Caradoc Evans*).

7 Russell Davies, 'Inside the "House of the Mad": the Social Context of Mental Illness, Suicide and the Pressures of Rural Life in South West Wales, c. 1860-1920', *Llafur: Journal of the Society for the Study of Welsh Labour History* 4, no. 2 (1985), pp. 20-35, explores the records of the Joint Counties Lunatic Asylum at Carmarthen (Evans's 'House of the Mad').

8 Ieuan Gwynedd Jones sheds light on this complex area in 'Language and Community in Nineteenth-century Wales', in *A People and a Proletariat: Essays in the History of Wales, 1780-1980*, ed. David Smith (1980), pp. 47-71. Seeing language as "the touchstone of both politics and religion", he explores the roles, actual and perceived, of Welsh and English at the turn of the century ("English was the language of infidelity and atheism" … "the language of socialism was English").

9 See Russell Davies, '"In a Broken Dream": Some Aspects of Sexual Behaviour and the Dilemmas of the Unmarried Mother in South West Wales, 1887-1914', *Llafur: Journal of the Society for the Study of Welsh Labour History* 3, no. 4 (1983), pp. 24-33.

10 See David Jenkins, *The Agricultural Community in South-West Wales at the Turn of the Twentieth Century* (1971). Chapters 2 and 3 provide the statistics for this paragraph.

11 Jenkins, *Agricultural Community,* p. 231.

A FATHER IN SION

On the banks of Avon Bern there lived a man who was a Father in Sion. His name was Sadrach, and the name of the farmhouse in which he dwelt was Danyrefail. He was a man whose thoughts were continually employed upon sacred subjects. He began the day and ended the day with the words of a chapter from the Book and a prayer on his lips. The Sabbath he observed from first to last; he neither laboured himself nor allowed any in his household to labour. If in the Seiet, the solemn, soul-searching assembly that gathers in Capel Sion on the nights of Wednesdays after Communion Sundays, he was entreated to deliver a message to the congregation, he often prefaced his remarks with, "Dear people, on my way to Sion I asked God what He meant".

This episode in the life of Sadrach Danyrefail covers a long period; it has its beginning on a March night with Sadrach closing the Bible and giving utterance to these words:

"May the blessing of the Big Man be upon the reading of His Word." Then, "Let us pray."

Sadrach fell on his knees, the open palms of his hands together, his elbows resting on the table; his eight children — Sadrach the Small, Esau, Simon, Rachel, Sarah, Daniel, Samuel, and Miriam — followed his example.

Usually Sadrach prayed fluently, in phrases not unworthy of the minister, so universal, so intimate his pleading: tonight he stumbled and halted, and the working of his spiritful mind lacked the heavenly symmetry of the mind of the godly; usually the note of abundant faith and childlike resignation rang grandly throughout his supplications: tonight the note was one of despair and gloom. With Job he compared himself, for was not the Lord trying His servant to the uttermost? Would the all-powerful Big Man, the Big Man who delivered the Children of Israel from the hold of the Egyptians, give him a morsel of strength to bear his cross? Sadrach reminded God of his loneliness. Man was born to be mated, even as the animals in the fields. Without mate man was like an estate without an overseer, or a field of ripe corn rotting for the reaping-hook.

Sadrach rose from his knees. Sadrach the Small lit the lantern which was to light him and Esau to their bed over the stable.

"My children," said Sadrach, "do you gather round me now, for have I not something to tell you?"

Rachel, the eldest daughter, a girl of twelve, with reddish cheeks and bright eyes, interposed with:

"Indeed, indeed, now, little father; you are not going to preach to us this time of night!"

Sadrach stretched forth his hand and motioned his children be seated.

"Put out your lantern, Sadrach the Small," he said. "No, Rachel, don't you light the candle. Dear ones, it is not the light of this earth we need, but the light that comes from above."

"Iss, iss," Sadrach the Small said. "The true light. The light the Big Man puts in the hearts of those who believe, dear me."

"Well spoken, Sadrach the Small. Now be you all silent awhile, for I have things of great import to tell you. Heard you all my prayer?"

"Iss, iss," said Sadrach the Small.

"Sadrach the Small only answers. My children, heard you all my prayer? Don't you be blockheads now — speak out."

"There's lovely it was," said Sadrach the Small.

"My children?" said Sadrach.

"Iss, iss," they answered.

"Well, well, then. How can I tell you?" Sadrach put his fingers through the thin beard which covered the opening of his waistcoat, closed his eyes, and murmured a prayer. "Your mother Achsah is not what she should be. Indeed to goodness, now, what disgrace this is! Is it not breaking my heart? You did hear how I said to the nice Big Man that I was like Job? Achsah is mad."

Rachel sobbed.

"Weep you not, Rachel. It is not for us to question the all-wise ways of the Big Man. Do you dry your eyes on your apron now, my daughter. You, too, have your mother's eyes. Let me weep in my solitude. Oh, what sin have I committed, that God should visit this affliction on me?"

Rachel went to the foot of the stairs.

"Mam!" she called.

"She will not hear you," Sadrach interrupted. "Dear me, have I not put her in the harness loft? It is not respectable to let her out. Twm Tybach would have sent his wife to the madhouse of Carmarthen. But that is not Christian. Rachel, Rachel, dry your eyes. It is not your fault that Achsah is mad. Nor do I blame Sadrach the Small, nor Esau, nor Simon, nor Sarah, nor Daniel, nor Samuel, nor Miriam. Goodly names have I given you all. Live you up to them. Still, my sons and daughters, are you not all responsible for Achsah's condition? With the birth of each of you she has got worse and worse. Childbearing has made her foolish. Yet it is un-Christian to blame you."

Sadrach placed his head in his arms.

Sadrach the Small took the lantern and he and Esau departed for their bed over the stable; one by one the remaining six put off their clogs and crept up the narrow staircase to their beds.

Wherefore to her husband Achsah became as a cross, to her children as one forgotten, to everyone living in Manteg and in the several houses scattered on the banks of Avon Bern as Achsah the madwoman.

The next day Sadrach removed the harness to the room in the dwelling-house in which slept the four youngest children; and he put a straw mattress and a straw pillow on the floor, and on the mattress he spread three sacks; and these were the furnishings of the loft where Achsah spent her time. The frame of the small window in the roof he nailed down, after fixing on the outside of it three solid bars of iron of uniform thickness; the trap-door he padlocked, and the key of the lock never left his possession. Achsah's food he himself carried to her twice a day, a procedure which until the coming of Martha some time later he did not entrust to other hands.

Once a week when the household was asleep he placed a ladder from the floor to the loft, and cried:

"Achsah, come you down now."

Meekly the woman obeyed, and as her feet touched the last rung Sadrach threw a cow's halter over her shoulders, and drove her out into the fields for an airing.

Once, when the moon was full, the pair were met by Lloyd the Schoolin', and the sight caused Mishtir Lloyd to run like a frightened dog, telling one of the women of his household that Achsah, the madwoman, had eyes like a cow's.

At the time of her marriage Achsah was ten years older than her husband. She was rich, too: Danyrefail, with its stock of good cattle and a hundred acres of fair land, was her gift to the bridegroom. Six months after the wedding Sadrach the Small was born. Tongues wagged that the boy was a child of sin. Sadrach answered neither yea nor nay. He answered neither yea nor nay until the first Communion Sabbath, when he seized the bread and wine from Old Shemmi and walked to the Big Seat. He stood under the pulpit, the fringe of the minister's Bible-marker curling on the bald patch on his head.

"Dear people," he proclaimed, the silver-plated wine cup in one hand, the bread plate in the other, "it has been said to me that some of you think Sadrach the Small was born out of sin. You do not speak truly. Achsah, dear me, was frightened by the old bull. The bull I bought in the September fair. You, Shemmi, you know the animal. The red-and-white bull. Well, well, dear people, Achsah was shocked by him. She was running away from him, and as she crossed the threshold of Danyrefail, did she not give birth to Sadrach the Small? Do you believe me now, dear people. As the Lord liveth, this is the truth. Achsah, Achsah, stand you up now, and say you to the congregation if this is not right."

Achsah, the babe suckling at her breast, rose and murmured: "Sadrach speaks the truth."

Sadrach ate of the bread and drank of the wine.

Three months after Achsah had been put in the loft Sadrach set out at daybreak on a journey to Aberystwyth. He returned late at night, and, behold, a strange woman sat beside him in the horse car; and the coming of this strange woman made life different in Danyrefail. Early in the day she was astir, bustling up the children, bidding them fetch the cows, assist with the milking, feed the pigs, or do whatever work was in season.

Rachel rebuked Sadrach, saying, "Little father, why for cannot I manage the house for you? Indeed now, you have given to Martha the position that belongs to me, your eldest daughter."

"What mean you, my dear child?" returned Sadrach. "Cast you evil at your father? Turn you against him? Go you and read your Commandments."

"People are whispering," said Rachel. "They do even say that you will not be among the First Men of the Big Seat"

"Martha is a gift from the Big Man," answered Sadrach. "She has been sent to comfort me in my tribulation, and to mother you, my children."

"Mother!"

"Tut, tut, Rachel," said Sadrach, "Martha is only a servant in my house."

Rachel knew that Martha was more than a servant. Had not her transfer letter been accepted by Capel Sion, and did she not occupy Achsah's seat in the family pew? Did she not, when it was Sadrach's turn to keep the minister's month, herself on each of the four Saturdays take a basket laden with a chicken, two white-hearted cabbages, a peck of potatoes, a loaf of bread, and half a pound of butter to the chapel house of Capel Sion? Did she not drive with Sadrach to market and fair and barter for his butter and cheese and cattle and what not? Did she not tell Ellen the Weaver's Widow what cloth to weave for the garments of the children of Achsah?

These things Martha did; and Danyrefail prospered exceedingly: its possessions spread even to the other side of Avon Bern. Sadrach declared in the Seiet that the Lord was heaping blessings on the head of His servant. Of all who worshipped in Sion none was stronger than the male of Danyrefail; none more respected. The congregation elected him to the Big Seat. Sadrach was a tower of strength unto Sion.

But in the wake of his prosperity lay vexation. Rachel developed fits; while hoeing turnips in the twilight of an afternoon she shivered and fell, her head resting in the water ditch that is alongside the hedge. In the morning Sadrach came that way with a load of manure.

"Rachel fach," he said, "wake you up now. What will Martha say if you get ill?"

He passed on.

When he came back Rachel had not moved, and Sadrach drove away, without noticing the small pool of water which had gathered over the girl's head. Within an hour he came again, and said:

"Rachel, Rachel, wake you up. There's lazy you are."

Rachel was silent. Death had come before the milking of the cows. Sadrach went to the end of the field and emptied his cart of the manure. Then he turned and cast Rachel's body into the cart, and covered it with a sack, and drove home, singing the hymn which begins:

> "Safely, safely gather'd in,
> Far from sorrow, far from sin,
> No more childish griefs or fears,
> No more sadness, no more tears;
> For the life so young and fair
> Now hath passed from earthly care;
> God Himself the soul will keep,
> Giving His beloved — sleep."

Esau was kicked by a horse, and was hurt to his death; six weeks later Simon gashed his thumb while slicing mangolds, and he died. Two years went by, by the end of which period Old Ianto, the gravedigger of Capel Sion, dug three more graves for the children of Sadrach and Achsah; and over these graves Sadrach and Martha lamented.

But Sadrach the Small brought gladness and cheer to Danyrefail with the announcement of his desire to wed Sara Ann, the daughter of Old Shemmi. Martha and Sadrach agreed to the union provided Old Shemmi gave to his daughter a stack of hay, a cow in calf, a heifer, a quantity of bedclothes, and four cheeses. Old Shemmi, on his part, demanded with Sadrach the Small ten sovereigns, a horse and a cart, and a bedstead.

The night before the wedding Sadrach drove Achsah into the fields, and he told her how the Big Man had looked with goodwill upon Sadrach the Small, and was giving him Sara Ann to wife.

What occurred in the loft over the cowshed before dawn crept in through the window with the iron bars I cannot tell you. God can. But the rising sun found Achsah crouching behind one of the hedges of the lane that brings you from Danyrefail to the tramping road, and there she stayed, her eyes peering through the foliage, until the procession came by: first Old Shemmi and Sadrach, with Sadrach the Small between them; then the minister of Capel Sion and his wife; then the men and the women of the congregation; and last came Martha and Sara Ann.

The party disappeared round the bend: Achsah remained.

"Goodness me," she said to herself. "There's a large mistake now. Indeed, indeed, mad am I."

She hurried to the gateway, crossed the road and entered another field, through which she ran as hard as she could. She came to a hedge, and waited.

The procession was passing.

Sadrach and Sadrach the Small.

Achsah doubled a finger.

Among those who followed on the heels of the minister was Miriam.

Achsah doubled another finger.

The party moved out of sight: Achsah still waited.

"Sadrach the Small and Miriam!" she said, spreading out her doubled-up fingers. "Two. Others? Esau. Simon. Rachel. Sarah. Daniel. Samuel. Dear me, where shall I say they are? Six. Six of my children. Mad, mad am I?". . . . She laughed. "They are grown, and I didn't know them."

Achsah waited the third time for the wedding procession. This time she scanned each face, but only in the faces of Sadrach the Small and Miriam did she recognise her own children. She threw herself on the grass. Esau and Simon and Rachel, and Sarah and Daniel and Samuel. She remembered the circumstances attending the birth of each. . . . And she had been a good wife. Never once did she deny Sadrach his rights. So long as she lasted she was a woman to him.

"Sadrach the Small and Miriam," she said.

She rose and went to the graveyard. She came to the earth under which are Essec and Shan, Sadrach's father and mother, and at a distance of the space of one grave from theirs were the graves of six of the children born of Sadrach and Achsah. She parted the hair that had fallen over her face, and traced with her fingers the letters which formed the names of each of her six children.

. . . . .

As Sara Ann crossed the threshold of Danyrefail, and as she set her feet on the flagstone on which Sadrach the Small is said to have been born, the door of the parlour was opened and a lunatic embraced her.

A HEIFER WITHOUT BLEMISH

Deio and Katto Parcdu had been entertaining Job of the Stallion. Having made an end to eating, and Job and his stallion having taken to the road, Deio lifted his voice:

"Tomos, come you in here now."

Tomos passed over the earthen floor of the kitchen, and discarded his clogs on the threshold of the lower end, which is the parlour.

"Job of the old Stallion does say that Enoch Dinas has taken a farm near the shore of Morfa," said Deio.

"Indeed, now, there's a daft boy bach!" exclaimed Tomos. "What say you does Enoch want to do that for! Sure me, Dinas is as much as he can manage."

"Is not that what Job did say?" spoke Katto.

"Dinas is a fairish farm," said Deio. "Out of his old head is Enoch to leave it."

"Sad is Enoch's lot," said Katto. "A high female is his wife. And an unprofitable madam is the female."

"Iss, iss," said Deio. "She is a burden on the place. Where is the sense now in Enoch keeping a wife and a servant?"

"Enoch is head-stiff," said Katto. "Did not everyone tell him before he married that he would have to keep a servant? For why, dear me, did the iob marry such a useless woman?

What is the matter with the female? She brought with her nothing to Dinas."

"Look you at the wife of Tydu," said Deio gravely. "Isn't she a sampler?"

"She's as useful as a male about the place," added Katto.

"And she works like a black bach. And Evan her husband is always in his place in the meeting for prayer."

"Religion comes before all with Evan," said Deio.

"Large money indeed he puts in the Post Office," Katto went on. "Mistress Morgan of the Post does say that he's got thirty yellow sovereigns there now. What pity Tomos cannot find a woman like her."

Tomos came near to the round table, and bending his crooked body, spat into the fire.

"Think you now of Sara Jane the daughter of old Simon—" he began.

"Boy bach foolish!" cried Katto. "What nonsense you talk out of the back of your head! Sober serious, mouth not that you have thrown gravel at Sara Jane's window! She's not worth her broth."

"Katto is right," Deio put in. "There was me and Katto talking about renting Dinas for you if you could find a thrifty, tidy female."

"How voice you then about Gwen the widow of Noah?" asked Tomos. "There's a one she is for tending to the house!"

"You would have to pay her," said Deio. "It is not someone to look after the house you want. You need a woman to look after the land, and the cattle, and your milk, man. And after you. A woman who will be profitable. Sara Jane, indeed! No, boy bach, don't you deal lightly with Old Simon's wench. Not respectable is that to Capel Sion."

"Your father speaks sense, Tomos nice," said Katto. "It's time you wedded. Do you look round you for one like the wife of Tydu. Is she not tidy and saving? Was she not carting dung into the field when she was full? You will be five over forty in the eleventh month."

Deio took out from his mouth the tobacco that was therein and placed it on the table, and he also emptied his mouth of its tainted spittle. "Be you restful now, folk bach," he said, "for am I not going to speak about religion?" Then he raised his face and sang after the manner of the Welsh preacher: "Me and your mam are full of years, and the hearse from Capel Sion will soon take us home to the Big Man's Palace — a home, Tomos, where we will wear White Shirts, and where there is no old rent to pay. Tomos, Tomos, weepful you will be when I am up above. Little Great One, keep an eye on Tomos. Be with you son in Capel Sion. Amen."

When he had made an end, he put the tobacco back into his mouth, and he said: "One hundred and half a hundred sovereigns is the mortgage on Parcdu now."

"Do you listen, Tomos bach," Katto counselled her son.

"Go you off yourself tomorrow to the April Fair to search for a woman," said Deio.

Tomos said: "Iss, iss, indeed, then."

"And take you a cask of butter with you," said Katto. "Leave you the butter in the back of the old trap till your eyes have fallen upon a maid; and when she has found favour with you, ask her to sell for you the butter. If she has got a sharp tongue in her mouth and makes a good bargain, say to her that you will marry her, but if she is not free of tongue, say you nothing more to her, but go in search of another."

Deio spoke: "Tell her your father sits in the Big Seat in Sion, in the parish of Troedfawr, in Shire Cardigan. As earnest of your intention say that you are commanded to buy a heifer to start life with in Dinas. Now, little son, don't you say anything about the old mortgage."

Tomos promised to observe his father's instructions.

"Get you there early in the morning, then," his father said to him. "Put the black mare in the car. And, Tomos, don't you give a ride to anybody, for fear those old robbers of excisemen will catch you."

"Make yourself comely," said Katto. "And when you get there, put out your belly largely. See too that you get a heifer without blemish."

Tomos shaved his chin and his long upper lip and combed his side whiskers, and he put axle-grease on his boots, and clothed himself in his Sabbath garments of homespun cloth; and harnessing the black mare to the car, in the back of which he placed a cask full of butter, he set out for the Fair of the month of April. Tomos got out of the car at Penrhiw, as the ascent therefrom into Castellybryn is rocky and steep, and guided the mare by the bridle. At the foot of the hill — this morning a street of many people and much cattle — he turned into the yard of the Drivers' Arms.

"Fair morning, Tomos the son of Deio," said the ostler of the Drivers' Arms to him.

"Say have you an empty stall, little son?" Tomos asked.

"Surely."

"Fair morning, Tomos. How was you, man? And how was your old father?"

Tomos turned round and looked into the face of Job of the Stallion.

"Quite well, thanks be to you, Job bach."

"What's your errand, boy bach? Old Deio your father did not say anything the day before today."

Job, his small feet planted close together underneath his bandy legs, gazed reproachfully at Tomos.

"Well-well," said Tomos, "am I not selling a cask of butter, man?"

"There's excuse for you now, dear me; old Katto must be mad to send you with a cask of butter to the fair. Now, now, Tomos, do you mouth to me then your errand quick at once."

"For what you don't know that Dinas is going, man?" replied Tomos.

"But, Tomos, why act so foolish? Was not me that told old Deio about it?"

"Of course. Father wants me to take it."

"Little Tomos, do you speak plainly. I am not curious, but what in the name of goodness are you doing here? Be you immediate, for have I not a lot of business to do?"

"Job of the Stallion, why you are so hasty for, man? Look you, indeed, I am come for a wife."

Job pouted his lips reprovingly, and he squeezed the large, cracked mole which was between his eyebrows with forefinger and thumb.

"I blame you, Tomos, for being so secret about your affairs."

He thought.

"Dango!" he exclaimed. "There's Nell Blaenffos. Do you know Nell, Tomos?"

"Nell Blaenffos?"

"You are as stupid as a frog, man. Blaenffos. Near Henllan. Nell the daughter of Sam."

"Is she a tidy wench?"

"For why you make me savage, Tomos? Nell is Sam's only child. She is here with her old father paying off the last of the mortgage."

Job shouted across the yard into the inn: "Is Nell Blaenffos there?"

"Dammo!" came the reply. "She was here this one minute. Nell Blaenffos! Nell Blaenffos!"

Many voices repeated the call. They cried: "Nell Blaenffos!

Nell Blaenffos! Job of the Stallion wants you."

The cry was taken up by folk standing on the doorstep, and it reached a group of men and women gossiping in the middle of the roadway. "Nell fach," said one of the group, "is not old Job of the Stallion needing you?"

"For shame!" observed a ponderous-waisted woman. "What for you are thinking? For shame, Nell Blaenffos!"

The people laughed.

"Go you, little daughter," said the large woman, "and see what that old Job needs you for."

Nell — stout and red of face, and puffing — appeared before Job, and Job informed her that Tomos begotten of Deio Parcdu (this Deio being the strongest farmer in the parish of Troedfawr, and the saintliest man in the Big Seat in Capel Sion) was desirous of taking her into his bed.

Tomos nodded his head, and said: "Iss-iss. How was you, Nell fach?"

Nell proved him with questions.

Job took Tomos to a corner in the yard, and held a whispered conversation with him; returning he told Nell that Dinas, a farm of sixty acres, was to be let, that Deio was prepared to perform his share in stocking the farm, that as earnest of this Tomos was authorised that day to buy a heifer for Dinas.

"You see, Nell fach, that you will have to be quick, or else the best cattle will be sold," said Job.

"Dear, dear, now," said Tomos, "I had forgotten the old cask of butter I have to sell."

"There, indeed!" said Job. "Go off you two together and sell the cask and talk this thing over. Remember when you settle down in Dinas that my Stallion bach is to serve your first mare. Thus you will pay me for this."

Tomos lifted the cask out of the car and placed it on Nell's shoulder, and he followed Nell to the place where butter merchants assemble. One dealer came and offered tenpence three-farthings a pound; for him Nell refused to remove even the cloth from the mouth of the cask. Another came and offered tenpence half-penny; in reply to him Nell said: "Go your way, you fool. You would rob me pure." Now the dealer was a young man, who did not know the ways of Castellybryn, and he was aware that the first dealer was a big buyer and a cunning bargainer; so he purchased the butter for elevenpence farthing a pound, being a farthing a pound above the market price of that day.

Tomos took the money and tied his handkerchief over it, and he bought a penny cake, and while he was eating it he said to Nell:

"How speak you about Dinas?"

"Is the land well watered?" asked Nell.

"Iss, indeed."

"Is there water in the close?"

"Well, well, not in the close, Nell fach, but at the bottom of the field under the house."

"Mouth you now about the outhouses."

"Enoch had a new roof put over the stable when he went there four years ago."

"How much money has your father Deio got?"

"Now you've asked me a puzzle, Nell fach. I don't know, for sure!"

"Is Parcdu his?"

"Indeed it is."

"Is it mortgaged?"

"Not for a red penny, Nell Blaenffos."

"How many brothers and sisters have you got?"

"Not one, Nell fach."

"Come you back with me to the Drivers' and mouth to old

father."

Sam Blaenffos had already seen Job of the Stallion and had conversed with him, and he had been told nothing except that which was good about Deio Parcdu and his son Tomos.

"When is the wedding to be, little son?" Sam asked Tomos.

"What say you now?"

"There's plenty of time to discuss that," said Sam. "Tell you old Deio to meet me here next market day, and we will arrange matters."

"I will indeed, man," replied Tomos.

"Goodbye now, and good-bye to your father as well," said Sam.

Tomos turned his back on the Drivers' Arms, and on Nell Blaenffos, and on the father of Nell Blaenffos, and with a hand in the pocket of his coat and a hand in the pocket of his trousers he moved slowly in and out among the cattle. The fingers of the clock over the door of the surgery of Dr Morgan pointed to fifteen minutes past ten, wherefore Tomos bent his shoulders and rebuked himself:

"The morning is far spent. And there's a small bit of work I've done!"

When he came that way again the fingers of the clock pointed to twenty-five minutes past five in the afternoon, and there was a pleasing smile in his face, for was he not leading on a halter a heifer without blemish?

THE WAY OF THE EARTH

Simon and Beca are waiting for Death. The ten acres of land over Penrhos — their peat-thatched cottage under the edge of the moor — grows wilder and weedier. For Simon and Beca can do nothing now. Often the mood comes on the broken, helpless old man to speak to his daughter of the only thing that troubles him.

"When the time comes, Sara Jane fach," he says, "don't you hire the old hearse. Go you down to Dai the son of Mali, and Isaac the Cobbler, and Dennis the larger servant of Dan, and Twm Tybach, and mouth you like this to them: 'Jasto, now, my little father Simon has gone to wear the White Shirt in the Palace. Come you then and carry him on your shoulders nice into Sion.'"

"Yea, Sara fach," Beca says, "and speak you to Lias the Carpenter that you will give no more than ten over twenty shillings for the coffin."

Simon adds: "If we perish together, make you one coffin serve."

Neither Simon nor Beca has further use for life. Paralysis shattered the old man the day of Sara Jane's wedding; the right side of his face sags, and he is lame on both his feet. Beca is blind, and she gropes her way about. Worse than all, they stand without the gates of Capel Sion — the living sin of all the land: they were married after the birth of Sara Jane, and though in the years of their passion they were all that a man and woman can be to each other, they begat no children. But Sion, jealous that not even his errant sheep shall lie in the parish graveyard and swell in appearance those who have worshipped the fripperies of the heathen Church, will embrace them in Death.

The land attached to Penrhos was changed from sterile moorland into a fertile garden by Simon and Beca. Great toil went to the taming of these ten acres of heather into the most fruitful soil in the district. Sometimes now Simon drags himself out into the open and complains when he sees his garden; and he calls Beca to look how the fields are going back to heatherland. And Beca will rise from her chair and feel her way past the bed which stands against the wooden partition, and as she touches with her right hand the ashen post that holds up the forehead of the house she knows she is facing the fields, and she too will groan, for her strength and pride are mixed with the soil.

"Sober serious, little Simon," she says, "this is the way of the earth, man bach."

But she means that it is the way of mortal flesh . . . of her daughter Sara Jane, who will no longer give the land the labour it requires to keep it clean and good. Sara Jane has more than she can do in tending to her five-year-old twins and her dying parents, and she lets the fields pass back into wild moorland.

In the days of his sin and might Simon had been the useful man of Manteg. He was careless then that the gates of Sion were closed against him. He possessed himself of a cart and horse, and became the carrier between the cartless folk of Manteg and the townspeople of Castellybryn, eight miles down the valley. He and Beca saved; oil lamp nor candle never lit up their house, and they did not spend money on coal because peat was to he lifted just beyond their threshold. They stinted themselves in half-pennies, gathered the pennies till they amounted to shillings, put the silver in a box till they had five sovereigns' worth of it, and this sum Simon took to the bank in Castellybryn on his next carrier's journey. They looked to the time their riches would triumph over even Sion and so open for them the gates of the temple.

As soon as the Schoolin' allowed her to leave the Board School, Sara Jane was made to help Beca in all the farm work, thus enabling Simon to devote himself almost entirely to his neighbours. The man was covetous, and there were murmurings that strange sheaves of wheat were threshed on his floor, that his pigs fattened on other people's meal.

In accordance with the manner of labouring women Sara Jane wore clogs which had iron rims beneath them, grey stockings of coarse wool that were patched on the heels and legs with artless darns, and short petticoats; in all seasons her hands were chapped and ugly. Still with her auburn hair, her firm breast, and her white teeth, she was the desire of many. Farm servants ogled her in public places; farmers' sons lay in wait for her in lonely places. Men spoke to her frankly, and with counterfeit smiles in their faces; Sara Jane answered their lustful sayings with lewd laughter, and when the attack became too pressing she picked up her petticoats and ran home. Nor was she put out over the attentions she received: she was well favoured and she liked to be desired; and in the twilight of an evening her full-bosomed, ripe beauty struck Simon suddenly as he met her in the close. Her eyes were dancing with delight, and her breast heaving. Sadrach the Small had chased her right to Penrhos.

Simon and Beca discussed this that had happened, and became exceedingly afraid for her.

"There's an old boy, dear me, for you indeed!" said Simon.

"The wench fach is four over twenty now, and fretful I feel."

"Iss, iss, Simon," said Beca.

"If she was wedded now, she would be out of harm."

"Wisdom you mouth, Simon. Good, serious me, to get her a male."

"How say you then about Josi Cwmtwrch?"

"Clap your old lips, little man. Josi Cwmtwrch! What has Josi to give her? What for you talk about Josi?"

"Well, well, then. Tidy wench she is, whatever. And when we go she'll have the nice little yellow sovereigns in the bank."

Beca interrupted: "The eggs fetched three and ten pennies. Another florin now, Simon, and we've got five yellow sovereigns."

"Don't say then! Pity that is. Am I not taking the old Schoolin's pig to Castellybryn on Friday too? Went you to all the old nests, woman fach?"

"Iss, man."

"What is old Rhys giving for eggs now?"

"Five pennies for six. Big is the fortune the cheater is making."

Beca dropped off her outer petticoat and drew a shawl over her head, and she got into bed; an hour later she was followed by Simon. In the morning she took to Shop Rhys three shillings' worth of eggs.

This was the slack period between harvests, and Sara Jane went with Simon to Castellybryn; and while Simon was weighing the Schoolin's pig she wandered hither and thither, and going over the bridge which spans Avon Teify she paused at the window of Jenkins Shop General, attracted thereto by the soaps and perfumes that were displayed.

"How you are?" said a young man at her side.

"Man bach, what for you fright me?" said Sara Jane. She was moved to step away, for she had heard read that the corners of streets are places of great temptation. The young man — a choice young man and comely: he wore spectacles, had the front of his hair trimmed in waves, and his moustaches ended in thin points — the young man seized her arm.

"Free you are, boy bach," Sara Jane cried. "Go you on now!"

"Come you in and take a small peep at my shop," said the young man. . . .

When Sara entered her father's cart she had hidden in the big pocket of her under-petticoat a cake of scented soap and a bottle of perfume.

That night she extracted the hobnails out of the soles of her Sabbath boots. That night also she collected the eggs, and for every three she gathered she concealed one. This she did for two more days, and the third day she purchased a blouse in Shop Rhys. For this wastefulness her parents' wrath was kindled against her. The next Sunday she secretly used scented soap on her face and hands and poured perfume on her garments; and towards evening she traversed to the gateway where the moorland road breaks into the tramping way which takes you to Morfa-on-the-Sea. William Jenkins was waiting for her, his bicycle against the hedge; he was cutting the letters of his name into the gatepost. On the fourth night Sara Jane lay awake in bed. She heard the sound of gravel falling on the window pane, and she got up and let in the visitor.

The rumour began to be spread that William Jenkins, Shop General, was courting in bed with the wench of Penrhos, and it got to the ears of Simon and Beca.

"What for you want to court William Shinkins, Shop General, in bed for?" said Simon.

"There's bad you are," said Beca.

"Is not Bertha Daviss saying that he comes up here on his old iron horse?" said Simon.

"Indeed to goodness," answered Sara Jane, "what is old Bertha doing out so late for? Say she to you that Rhys Shop was with her?"

"Speak you with sense, wench fach," Beca said to her daughter.

"Is not William Shinkins going to wed me then?" said Sara Jane.

"Glad am I to hear that," said Simon. "Say you to the boy bach: 'Come you to Penrhos on the Sabbath, little Shinkins.'"

"Large gentleman is he," said Sara Jane.

"Of course, dear me," said Simon. "But voice you like that to him."

The Sabbath came, and people on their way to Capel Sion saw William Jenkins go up the narrow Roman road to Penrhos, and they said one to another: "Close will be the bargaining." Simon was glad that Sara Jane had found favour in William's eyes: here was a godly man and one of substance; he owned a Shop General, his coat was always dry, and he wore a collar every day in the week, and he received many red pennies in the course of a day. Simon took him out on the moor.

"Shall we talk this business then at once?" Mishtir Jenkins observed. "Make plain Sara Jane's inheritance."

"Much, little boy."

"Penrhos will come to Sara Jane, then?"

"Iss, man."

"Right that is, Simon. Wealthy am I. Do I not own Shop General? Man bach, there's a grand business for you!"

"Don't say!"

"Move your tongue now about Sara Jane's wedding portion," said Mishtir Jenkins.

"Dear me, then, talk will I to Beca about this thing," answered Simon.

Three months passed by. Sara Jane moaned because that her

breast was hurtful. Beca brewed for her camomile tea, but the pains did not go away. Then at the end of a day Sara Jane told Beca and Simon how she had done.

"Concubine!" cried Beca.

"Harlot!" cried Simon.

"For sure me, disgrace is this," said Beca.

Sara Jane straightened her shoulders.

"Samplers bach nice you are!" she said maliciously. "Crafty goats you are. What did the old Schoolin' use to say when he called the names in the morning? 'Sara Jane, the bastard of Simon and Beca.' Iss, that's the old Schoolin'. But William Shinkins will wed me. I shan't be cut out of the Seiet."

Simon and Beca were distressed.

"Go you down, little Simon, and word to the boy," said Beca.

"I've nothing to go for," replied Simon.

"Hap Madlen Tybach need coal?"

"No-no. Has she not much left? Did I not look upon the coal when I fetched the eggs?"

"Sorrowful it is you can find no errand. Wise would be to speech to the male bach."

"Dear little me! I'll go round and ask the tailor if he is expecting parcels from the station."

"Do you now. You won't be losing money if you can find a little errand."

At dawn Simon rose and went to Castellybryn. In going over the bridge of Avon Teify he halted and closed his eyes and prayed. This is his prayer: "Powerful Big Man bach, deal you fair by your little servant. And if Shinkins, Shop General, says, 'I am not the father of your wench's child,' strike him dead. We know he is. Ask you Bertha Daviss. Have we not seen his name on the gatepost? This, Jesus bach, in the name of the little White Jesus."

Outside Shop General he called in a loud voice: "William Shinkins, where he is?" Then he came down and walked into the parlour where Mishtir Jenkins was eating.

Simon said: "Sara Jane is with child."

"And say you do that to me," said Mishtir Jenkins.

"Iss, iss, man. Sore is Beca about it."

"Don't you worry, Simon bach, the time is long."

"Mishtir Shinkins. There's religious he is," said Simon, addressing William Jenkins in the third person, as is the custom in West Wales when you are before your betters. "Put him up the banns now then."

"I will, Simon."

"Tell he me, when shall I say to Beca thus: 'On such and such a day is the wedding'? Say him a month this day?"

"All right, Simon. I'll send the old fly from the Drivers' Arms to bring you and Sara Jane. Much style there will be. Did you voice to Beca about the matter?"

"What was that now, indeed, Mishtir Shinkins?"

"Why was you so dull? Sara Jane's portion, old boy."

"Well-well, iss. Well-well, no. We're poor in Penrhos, Mishtir Shinkins. Poor."

"Grudging you are with your money, Simon Penrhos."

"Don't he say like that. Make speech will I again with Beca."

Mishtir Jenkins stretched his face towards Simon, and said:

"What would you say, Simon, if I asked you to give me Sara Jane's portion this one small minute?"

"Waggish is his way, little Shinkins bach," said Simon with pretended good humour.

"My father had a farm and sovereigns and a cow when he wedded."

"Open my lips to Beca I will about this," answered Simon.

"Good, very," replied Mishtir Jenkins. "I will say about the wedding, man, when you bring me Beca's words."

"Shinkins! Shinkins!"

"Leave you me half a hundred of pounds of Sara Jane's portion and I'll stand by my agreement."

"Joking he is, William Shinkins. Deal well we will by Sara Jane on the day of her wedding."

William Shinkins spoke presently. "I am not a man to go back on my promise to Sara Jane," he said. "And am I not one of respect?"

Simon went home and gave thanks unto God Who had imparted understanding to the heart of William Jenkins. But folks in Manteg declared that designing men crossed the river in search of females to wed. Sara Jane was no longer ashamed. She went about and abroad and wore daily the boots from which she had taken out the hobnails.

On the appointed day the fly came to Penrhos, and Simon and Sara Jane went away in it: and as they passed through Manteg Bertha Daviss cried: "People bach, tell you me where you are going."

Simon told her the glad news.

Bertha waved her hand, and she cried to the driver: "Boy nice, whip up, whip up, or you'll have another passenger to carry."

Mishtir Jenkins met Simon and Sara Jane at the door of the inn.

"Sara Jane," he said, "stop you outside while me and your father expound to each other."

He took Simon into the stable.

"Did you ask Beca about the yellow sovereigns?" he said.

"Iss, iss. Many sovereigns he will get."

"How many?"

"Shinkins bach, why for he hurry? Bad it looks."

"Sound the figures now, Simon."

"Ten yellow sovereigns, dear me."

"Simon Penrhos, you and your wench go home."

"William Shinkins, he knows that Sara Jane is full. I'll inform against him. The law of the Sessions I'll put on him. Indeed I will."

"Am I not making Sara Jane mistress of Shop General? Solemn me, serious it is to wed a woman with child!"

"There's hard he is, Shinkins. Take two over ten sovereigns and a little parcel of potatoes, and a few white cabbages, and many carrots."

"Is that your best offer, Simon?"

"It's all we have, little man. We're poor."

"Go with the wench. Costly the old fly is for me."

Simon seized Mishtir Jenkins' coat.

"William Shinkins bach," he cried, "don't he let his anger get the better of his goodness. Are we not poor? Accept he our daughter— "

"Simon Penrhos, one hundred of pounds you've got in the bank, man. Give me that one hundred this morning before the wedding. If you don't do that you shall see."

Simon shivered. He was parting with his life. It was his life and Beca's life. She had made it, turning over the heather, and wringing it penny by penny from the stubborn earth. He, too, had helped her. He had served his neighbours, and thieved from them. He wept.

"He asks too much," he cried. "Too much."

"Come, now, indeed," said William Jenkins. "Do you act religious by the wench fach."

Simon went with him to the bank, and with a smudge and a cross blotted out his account. Then he witnessed the completion of the bargain in Capel Baptists, which is beyond the Sycamore Tree.

The bridegroom took the bride home to Shop General, and he gave half of the dowry to a broker's man who had been put in possession. Some of the remaining fifty sovereigns went to his landlord for overdue rent, and on the rest William Jenkins and Sara Jane lived for nearly a year. Then the broker's man returned, wherefore William Jenkins gave over the fight and fled out of the land.

THE TALENT THOU GAVEST

Eben the son of Hannah held up his right arm and displayed the palm of his hand.

Mishtir Lloyd the Schoolin' said: "Put your old hand down now," and, gaping his mouth, proceeded to call out the register.

"Maggie Shones?"

"Here, iss."

"Eben Tomos?"

"Here, iss," answered three voices together.

"For what you do not shut your chins, you dirty cows!" said Mishtir Lloyd. "Why do you all act like old horses without any gumption! Now, then, Eben the Son of Sarah the daughter of Silah?"

"Here, iss."

"Eben, Mari's child by Job of the Stallion?"

"Here, iss."

"Eben the son of Hannah the widow of Will?"

"Here, iss."

Mishtir Lloyd called by name each of the eighty-five scholars on his register; when he came to the end, he said:

"What for was your hand up just now, man, Eben the son of Hannah?"

"Did I not want to tell him, little Mishtir, that I am not

coming to school any more then?" replied Eben.

"Dear me, dear me, now indeed you are not coming for why?"

"Mishtir bach, does he not know that I am going to the moor to mind the sheep of Shames?"

"Ho, and you say that?"

Mishtir Lloyd picked up his round ebony ruler and drew a straight line over Eben's name on the register.

The next morning at daybreak Eben, a crust of bread and a piece of cheese in his trousers pocket, was ready to take up his duties. Before he went Hannah addressed these words to him:

"Do you see now, little Eben, that none of Shames's old sheep go astray, for Shames is quick to anger. Don't you do any evil pranks against him, because it is not meet that Shames shall report us to the Big Man. Earn every mite of the shilling a week he gives you, Eben bach. Do we not need these pennies badly? Last year I sacrificed only three half-crowns to Sion. And for sure the Judge will inform the Great Male about me."

Eben, having walked over the mile and a half of heather, and having come to the point from which you can on a clear day see the waters of Cardigan Bay, opened the gate of the enclosure in which Shames's sheep spent the night.

This Eben did every day till he grew out of knee-breeches into long corduroy trousers. His life was lonely; books were closed against him, because he had not been taught to read; and the sense of the beautiful or the curious in Nature is slow to awake in the mind of the Welsh peasant. After a time Eben began to hold whispered conversations with himself. Gradually he found consolation in his voice, the sound of which fell pleasingly upon his ears. He knew many hymns by heart, and these hymns he recited to the shivering heather and the grazing sheep.

One afternoon, his legs dangling over the edge of the stone

quarry, he fell asleep, and in his dream the Big Man — a white-bearded, vigorous, stern, elderly giant, broad as the front of Capel Sion and taller than the roof — came to him, saying:

"Eben bach, why for now do you waste your days in sleep? Go you, little son, and dig a hole in the place where stood Old Shaci's hut."

"It'll be a big hole, little Big Man," answered Eben, "if I must make it the size of Old Shaci's hut."

The Big Man replied: "There's a boy you are for pleading! Go you up and stand against the sour apple tree with your face to the sea. At a distance of three steps from the trunk of the tree dig an old hole after the fashion of a grave."

"Do you tell me now for what?" Eben asked.

"For sure, is there not a talent buried there?"

Eben left Shames's sheep and came to Penrhos.

"Little Simon," he said, "lend you me an old pickaxe and a shovel."

Returning, he numbered the sheep, and drove them to the summit of the moor, and when he came to the mound on which a hundred years ago Old Shaci built his hut, he took off his coat and waistcoat, and dug a hole as deep as a grave and of the shape of a coffin. But he did not find anything.

That night the God of Capel Sion came to Eben again.

"Now that you have got the talent, Eben Bach, do you use it," He said.

"Dear little Big Man," answered Eben, "there's foolish you talk. Did I not dig till my old hands were covered with blisters? Provokeful you are."

The Big Man spoke: "Eben bach, here is the talent."

Eben opened his eyes. He sat up in bed and held out his hands: the dawn showed grey in his mother's face.

Weeks passed and months passed, and each night Eben said this prayer:

> "In God's name to my bed I go,
> God keep the hale and those in woe;
> I'll lay my body down to sleep,
> I'll give my soul to Christ to keep,
> And in the name of God I'll sleep."

Adding:

> "God did promise me a talent:
> Let Him show me what He meant."

Now in those days the ruler of Capel Sion was the Respected Bern-Davydd, famous throughout the land for his singing eloquence; thus oftentimes Eben sang the minister's sayings while he kept guard over Shames's sheep.

Understanding broke upon him suddenly.

"Dear, dear," he said to himself, "this is the talent the Great Male gave me. I am to be a preacher bach."

In the holiness of his joy he rose to his feet and sang:

"The dear Big Man has given His little servant a talent. Sheep bach that belong to Shames, what do you think the talent is now? He has called Eben the son of Hannah the widow woman of Will to preach the Fair Word. Wise indeed is the White Jesus to give His little servant the strength to sing the Gospel."

Eben came home and said to his mother Hannah:

"Mam fach, the talent the Almighty gave me is for preaching."

"Eben, why you are so vain?" Hannah said to him.

But Hannah published the news to the men who sat in the Big Seat in Capel Sion, so it came about that Old Bensha of the Road, in order to prove him, requested him to say a little prayer in the Seiet. Beautiful and songlike was the supplication that Eben offered: he sang mournfully for those at sea, for sinners that worshipped in places other than Capel Sion; he sang joyously for the First Men who occupied the high places, for the many blessings poured upon the congregation, for the Big Man's gift of His Son to judge over Sion.

Hannah clothed herself in her most respectful garments, which were black and decorated with ornaments of jet and flowers of crêpe, for this is the wear of the women whose constant thoughts are of Death and the burial of the dead; and she came down to the Shepherd's Abode, where dwelt the Respected Bern-Davydd.

"Eben bach," she said, "is talking about being a preacher."

"Religious hearing," said the Judge. "Have I not had sound of the boy's nice prayer?"

"Little holy respected," said Hannah, "good will it be if in his saintliness he lets a concert religious be held in the Capel so that Eben bach can be sent to College Carmarthen."

"Sure, indeed," answered Bern-Davydd. "I will cry from the pulpit: 'Buy each of you a ticket for Eben's concert. Two silver shillings is the price, people bach.'"

When Eben came away from College Carmarthen his holiness was voiced abroad the land and three Capels sent him word to come and rule over them. Of the three he distinguished the finger of God in the weakest — Capel Salem in Castellybryn. In the time of the respected Caleb Daviss it was said, "A fountain of light is Capel Salem"; but the godly Caleb ascended, whereof the glory departed and the tabernacle became as a withered roadside tree that harbours upon itself all the refuse the wind brings. Eben summoned the chief praying men into the Capel every night for thirty days, to entreat the Lord to restore the religious lustre of His tabernacle. Their prayers were answered: whereas at the beginning of Eben's ministry the congregation could be counted by the dozen, in two years their numbers were above any in the shire. His fame spread, and the people called him "Eben bach the Singer". People said of him: "He is exalted over all the judges."

But in the high day of his spiritual prosperity Eben's powers decreased: his discourses got to be less songlike, he conversed with rather than preached to his congregation, and he wrote out his sermons. Men and women murmured: "There's pity, now, dear me, about Eben bach the Singer."

The men of the Big Seat reproached him.

"Well-well, Eben bach, no one wept again the last Sunday," said Ben Shop Draper.

"Indeed to goodness, not one 'Hallelujah' or 'Amen' did I hear," said Noah Shop Boots and Clogs.

"For what he say that life is more than religion?" asked Ben.

"Little Ben and Noah," replied Eben, "the Palace must be here on earth."

Ben rose from his chair and said: "Eben bach, an old atheist he is."

"Were he not the ruler," said Noah, "pray for him I would this one night."

"Listen you to me now," said Eben. "I have not preached to you at all the real religion. I offered you the White Palace or the Fiery Pool. Men, men, that is not right. If you don't live in Heaven here you won't live in Heaven when you perish. Look you at Roberts of the Shop Grocer. Did he not make his servant Mari very full barely a year after he stood up in the Seiet and said that he prayed each night to be taken to Mistress Roberts? Did he not cry 'Hallelujah!' and 'Amen'?"

"Man, man, wrong you are to speak so about Roberts of the Shop Grocer," said Ben. "Poor Roberts bach was sorely tempted, and he is forgiven. And has he not sent the bad bitch about her business? Now think you over these things, and do you not be a blockhead to throw away your house and one hundred of sovereigns a year."

So Eben bach the Singer — short, square, stooping, bushy, sandy hair falling over his forehead and shoulders like a sheaf of straw — gave up his house, his one hundred sovereigns a year, and his charge, and he returned to the house of his mother. His name became a proverb and a byword. The deacons of Capel Sion prayed for him in private and in public, but the voice of the singer was silent.

On a day Ben Shop Draper journeyed to Hannah's cottage.

"Eben, Eben," he cried, "woeful is the errand I have to speech to you. The new ruler cannot keep the flock together."

"Ho, indeed."

"You have sinned hardly against Capel Salem, Eben bach."

"Don't you say that now."

"Iss, indeed. You took the temple in marriage. Now you have divorced her. The Big Man will count this serious against you, Eben. Dear me, one hundred sovereigns and a house, and eight Sabbaths off in the year."

"How could I preach against my conscience?" asked Eben.

"Look you not at things in that light, dear man. Suppose now we give you ten more sovereigns? Awake and gather yourself together, and ask the Big Man bach to show you the way."

People in the neighbourhood declared Eben was mad, that he had spewed on his own glory.

"Gird on your armour," remarked Lloyd the Schoolin' to him. "Pray to be rid of the Evil Spirit."

Eben made no answer.

"Wicked you are," proceeded Mishtir Lloyd. "Has not the Big Man given you a talent?"

"Iss, iss, for sure: He did give me a large talent."

"Shame upon you, you old cow, for throwing it against the Big Man's teeth."

"But I want to use it," retorted Eben. "The congregation

won't let me, Lloyd bach. So long as I employed half a talent all went well."

If at this time you happened to be taking the cart-road which cuts across the moor, past the quarry and Old Shaci's hut, you would have seen Eben sitting on the fringe of the heather.

Folk who came that way were in the habit of remarking to him:

"Glad day to you, Eben the son of Hannah."

Without lifting his eyes, Eben would reply:

"A glad day to you."

"What are you waiting for, man?"

"For the Angel of the Lord."

"Indeed to goodness now, how will you know him when he comes?"

"Sure me, I won't miss him."

The angel came towards the close of a day. Eben saw him, and greeting him with a wave of the hand, he hurried to Penrhos.

"Simon bach," he said, "do you now lend me your old pickaxe and shovel."

"Man, man," replied Simon, "foolish you are to begin a job this time of the night."

"He may not come this way again," answered Eben.

Eben hastened over the heather to the place where Old Shaci's hut was. Taking off his coat and his waistcoat, and loosening his braces, he dug a hole in the ground, a hole deep as a grave and of the shape of a coffin. In the darkness he stood over the open grave, his coat buttoned, india-rubber cuffs on his wrists, his hair, wet with perspiration, thrown back over his head.

"Big Lord," he spoke, "the talent Thou gavest me brought a great deal of woe with it. Let Thy angel here, O Big Man, bear witness now that I return to Thee Thy talent. And do Thou let me depart in peace, to make the best use I can of the half-talent which is mine . . ."

He opened his hands and spread his palms over the open grave, as though he dropped something into it; and having prayed he took off his coat, his waistcoat, and his india-rubber cuffs, and cast the earth back into the grave.

He returned to his mother's cottage, and he shaved off his beard, and brought forth from his box the black coat he wore in the pulpit; and in the morning he clothed himself in his preacher's raiment, and wrote this message:

"Beloved brothers in God of Capel Salem, which is in the Castellybryn:

Your judge has found the way. Hallelujah! Amen! Glory! Rejoice with me, my brothers. For I have found the true light. The light that shineth sinners to repentance! My brothers, God has told me to go forth into the vineyard. God has told me to resume my labours in Capel Salem. Pray, my beloved, that my labours will be very fruitful among you. Let not the matter of the little sovereigns engage your minds at this joyful time. Has not our dear brother Ben Shop Draper arranged all that?

Your Ruler in the faith,

EBEN."

THE GLORY THAT WAS SION'S

Twm Tybach was abhorred of Capel Sion. In all his acts he was evil. He was born out of sin, and he walked in the company of loose men. His features were fair, and he had a rakish eye, before which the heart of Madlen utterly melted. Now Madlen owned two pigs, a cow and a heifer, several heads of poultry, and Tybach, the stone-walled cottage that is beyond the Schoolhouse. In his fortieth year Twm coveted Madlen's possessions; and inasmuch as Madlen was on the borderline of her womanhood she received Twm's advances with joy. So Twm hired Old Shemmi's horse-car and drove Madlen to Castellybryn, where the two were married in the house of the registrar. The occasion is memorable to Madlen because that night she slept in a virgin's bed, her husband having gone into the bed of Old Mari who sold sweet loshins in the market place.

Thereon Twm lived on Madlen. He poached a little, but he was credited with more rabbits and hares than he would risk his liberty to trap; in season he pretended to help his neighbours in the hayfield, but nearly always succeeded in getting under covert with a woman.

He was as irreligious as an irreligious Welshman can be. He defied the Big Man openly; never except on market and fair days did he wear his best clothes; in passing the Respected

Josiah Bryn-Bevan and Mistress Bryn-Bevan he kept his cap on his head and whistled, and once he made Mistress Bryn-Bevan sick by spitting loudly on the ground; he frequented the inn which is kept by Mistress Shames, where he consorted with the disreputable Shon the Pig Drover — one without honour in the land.

Six weeks after his wedding Twm was stricken by illness. The Respected Josiah Bryn-Bevan, then Judge of Capel Sion, declared that the Lord was smiting His enemy, a just fate for all that offendeth Him. The third day of his illness Twm crept into the four-poster bed in the kitchen, and he ordered Madlen to bake a loaf of leavened bread and to place it on his belly; and a stubby beard grew on his chin.

The evening of that day Dr Morgan came by Tybach; Madlen stopped him, saying, "Indeed, now, doctor bach, come him in and give me small counsel about Twm."

The doctor examined Twm and he said to him: "Well-well, Twm, you will perish in a few days."

When Madlen heard this she placed a kettle of water on the fire and brought down her husband's razor from the highest shelf of the dresser.

Twm's face turned very white, for the man was afraid of Death.

"There's no chance for you, little Twm," the doctor said. "You are a hundred times worse than the boy in the Bible who took up his old bed and walked."

The account of how the days of the evil-favoured Twm Tybach were rounding on him was carried from mouth to mouth, and none was sorry. It was told to the Respected Josiah Bryn-Bevan in Shop Rhys. The teller of it was Bertha Daviss. This is what she said:

"Dear me! Dear me! The old calf of Twm Tybach is passing."

"Madlen will want mourning," said Rhys quickly. "She has not had a death for many years."

The Respected Josiah Bryn-Bevan was a religious man, and aware of Twm's evil reputation.

"Indeed to goodness," he said, with much solemnity. "And you do say so now, Miss Daviss?"

"Iss, iss," said Bertha, addressing the minister. "Man, man, why for he does not know that Twm Tybach is a Congregationalist? Was not old Eva his mother cut out of the Seiet when Twm was born? For sure me, that was so."

"What iobish do you spout, Bertha!" said Rhys. "What credit is the scamp unto Sion?"

"Be you merciful, little Rhys," returned the minister. "Do you forgive others as you need forgiveness."

"Maybe Twm is no credit," observed Bertha, "but we will have to bury him. Is not our graveyard the fullest in all the land?"

"You say wisely, Bertha Daviss," said the minister. "You say wisely, Bertha fach. Iss not the grave our last home then? We must begrudge it to no man. O little ones, there is largish space in the Big Man's acre."

"No, no, Respected bach," cried Bertha. "For why? The graveyard is full. Father was the last to be laid there. And in comfort did he go up when he knew of that glory."

Rhys Shop looked upon the minister. The minister looked upon Bertha: his gaze travelled from her clogs, her torn stockings and her turned-over petticoat to the yellow skin of her face and the narrow eyes which looked out damply over her bridgeless nose.

"Woman," he cried at last, "dost thou speak what thou knowest to be true, or dost thou repeat unto me — yea, unto me thy Judge — that which is idle gossip?"

"The truth, Bryn-Bevan bach. The truth."

The minister was confounded. The muscles of his cheeks moved nervously under his red beard. Then he arose and saying, "Fair day, boys bach," buttoned his frock-coat and grasped his varnished stick, and left the shop. Rhys and Bertha stood by, and when he was gone they stood in the way of the door and watched the high, thin, tall-hatted figure treading heavily clown the road towards Capel Sion; and at the week-night Meeting for Prayer everyone there knew that though the Respected Bryn-Bevan was blessed with much wisdom, understanding, and knowledge, the Big Man had loaded him with a burden heavy to bear.

Never within Capel Sion, nor within the boundaries of the parish, has been heard such a plea as that which was spoken by Bryn-Bevan that night. In the language of Adam and Eve he petitioned that his brother Twm Tybach would find repentance in the fulness of time, so that Death would find his putrid body cleansed and worthy of burial in the bosom of the new graveyard.

With the minister's amen, Abel Shones, the officer for poor relief, rose and suggested a deputation to wait upon the vicar seeking permission to inter Twm's body in the church graveyard.

"Very mad is Abel Shones, males bach," said Old Shemmi. "When Twm's sins are forgotten, the Church will claim him as her own."

"And possession, dear me, counts for much in the law," said Sadrach Danyrefail.

Lloyd the Schoolin' was for compromise.

"At the entrance to Capel Sion," he said, "we will put up an old stone on which is written these words: 'Tomos Tomos, Tybach, lieth not here. Tomos lieth in the parish church. Why, dear people? Because the graveyard of Capel Sion was so full that there was no room for further burials'."

"What's the use of a tombstone," asked Old Shemmi, "if there is nothing under it? Does a landless man go to Castellybryn to buy a plough?"

"O you people," the Respected Bryn-Bevan broke in, "you are all wandering on the moorness. Dear me. Dear me! Let us now seek deliverance from this trial which it has pleased God to inflict upon us. Let them who go to church — tithe gatherers and the like — be buried in church ground. Well do we know the fewness of graves there. We know where the Angel and the trumpet will be. Our graveyard, dear ones, is it not the glory of Sion? No, indeed then, we cannot spare one clay. Sit you down now and reason with one another."

"Very suitable," observed Old Shemmi, "is the field over Abel Shones's house."

"I am not afraid to enter the Palace," said Abel. "But, friends bach, does not my drinking-water come through that field?"

Wherefore the wrath of the minister waxed hot against Abel.

"None except a dirty old atheist," the Respected Bryn-Bevan said, "would bring materialism to bear upon a sacred subject. It is the water of life that matters, Abel Shones."

Great is the Respected Josiah Bryn-Bevan.

Abel protested against the use of parables in debate.

"Dost thou then not believe in the Parables?" shouted the minister. "Come ye now, speak. O man, man, where dost thou expect to go to when thou hast shuffled off thy carnal garments? Dost thou expect to wear the White Shirt?"

At the end of the Big Seat Abel Shones was praying for Old Shemmi; now as Shemmi saw and heard this thing he too fell on his knees and prayed for the cure of Twm Tybach. Lloyd the Schoolin', having taken off his boots, stood on the seat of his pew, asking God to repent of His intention of spoiling Capel

Sion as He had done with Sodom and Gomorrah. "Don't you now, little Big Man," he prayed, "be influenced either this way or that by their talk. Think you to yourself, they do not know what they do." To this day the hour that remark was uttered is a memorial to the occurrence, for the congregation turned their faces to the clock, whose hands they did not think would move again.

"Brethren" — Mishtir Bryn-Bevan's voice rose above the noises — "Brethren, at this moment Twm Tybach may be passing into the Pool."

The First Men saw that Bryn-Bevan's counsel was good, and they discussed and disputed, and it came to be that Old Shemmi's scheme was adopted.

This field belonged to the squire, who regarded anyone trading under the name of Nonconformist as a thief and a quibbler. In his dealings with this kind the squire acted through his lawyer, and therefore many days had to pass before the ground would be transferred to Capel Sion.

Meanwhile those who worshipped in Sion were commanded to pray without ceasing that Twm's life would not end until the new burial place came into Sion's possession. But in spite of all the prayers each hour seemed to take Twm nearer the parish church. Three times in one day Madlen laid her black gown over the foot of the bed; three times she took the razor out of its case.

Many came to Tybach and prayed by Twm's bedside; some came from a distance, and they arrived weary and refreshed themselves with tea which Madlen brewed for them; and every visitor brought a present. The sick man was tempted with offerings of tins of sardines and corned beef, jars of red cabbage pickles and home-made jams. Mistress Bryn-Bevan sent a bottle of rhubarb wine. The man was angry when he was told that it would not make anyone drunk. Every night Rhys

Shop came with a quarter of a pound of biscuits which he laid on the pillow, and he also brought with him samples of black materials which were suitable for mournful garments.

Even the Respected Josiah Bryn-Bevan came and stood over Twm's bed. Twm opened his eyes and said he thought his visitor was Shon the Pig Drover.

"Twm!" Madlen cried. "Shameful you are! There's a squirrel for you! Say something religious to our little Judge."

The minister sat on the window-sill and said: "Twm, indeed for sure, glad you ought to be, sinner bach, that you are to be laid in little Capel Sion."

If ever the minister was inclined to the sin of unbelief in deathbed repentance it was when he heard Twm's answer and saw Twm's face.

"O Twm," he said, "there's glory that is awaiting for you, man. After many years I will come to Capel Sion with my grandchildren and I will show them your grave and say to them, 'This is the grave of Tomos Tomos, Tybach. He was buried the day the graveyard was opened'."

But Twm hardened his heart and would not take any comfort from the words of the Ruler of Capel Sion.

"Shon bach," he whimpered, "would be nice to me."

"You have been a bad man, Twm," the minister sang. "But now you are coming into a heritage of splendour. Come forth from your house of bondage. I am your deliverer, and I will walk before your coffin, Twm bach, to your last home in Capel Sion."

Twm turned his face to the wall; and he tried to stuff his ears with the ends of the patchwork quilt that covered him.

The minister went away, and he said to his congregation:

"Be comforted. Twm will be buried in the new little burial-ground."

Time wore on. The title deeds of the new burial-ground

were made over to the First Men, and Capel Sion lifted his head and murmured, "The glory of Sion is not departed."

Although light flickered in the window of Tybach throughout several nights; although many saw the Candle of the Corpse — that spirit light which foretells death — going out of the house and along the road to Capel Sion; although Madlen herself heard the moan of the Spirit Hound, Twm did not die.

People did not come any more to Tybach, and the praying men ceased to pray for Twm; for they knew he would die, and whether he liked it or not his sinful bones would rest in the land that was the glory of Capel Sion.

Late one night Twm told Madlen to read to him about the man who took up his bed and walked. Barely had Madlen begun her reading than Twm groaned and gurgled.

"The end," said Madlen to herself. "Twm bach is in the Jordan."

She moved to the bed; Twm's eyes were opened. She closed them. His face was grey as if the Angel of Death had cast the down from his wings upon it.

The kettle was singing on the hob; Madlen shifted it on to the live coals, and she took the razor out of its case and stropped it on the leather which hung on the bedpost. Twm heard the hissing of the kettle, and he also heard the sound the flat of the blade made on the leather; and he understood. He put his fingers through the stubby beard which had grown on his chin. A fear came over him. He threw back the clothes which covered him, and wrapped around him the patchwork quilt, and he went and sat by the fire.

"Madlen!" he cried. "Little Madlen, is not the old kettle boiling then? There's slow mule you are! Come, make you a cup of tea now."

From first to last Twm's years were five-and-forty.

THE DEVIL IN EDEN

If ever the innermost meaning of the Word was in dispute in Capel Sion the Big Man sent an angel in a cloud with a message to Old Ianto of the Road, and this message Old Ianto interpreted to the congregation. Thus, honoured above men, Ianto got puffed up and vainglorious, whereat the Big Man sent a tempter to test him.

The tempter, in the flesh of a tramp, came to Manteg in the quiet of a Sabbath eve, and he found Ianto setting his thoughts in tune with Sion on the bank of the waters which are against the hedge of Abel Shones's garden.

The tramp stood over Old Ianto, and spoke to him:

"Tell you me now how far I am from the poorhouse of Castellybryn."

"Man, man," answered Ianto, "you're seven miles good and more."

Although it was then dusk the tempter made no move to pass on his journey.

"You seem weary, man bach," remarked Ianto.

"Indeed to goodness now, weary I am," answered the tramp.

"Sit you down and rest your little old feet," Ianto counselled him.

The tramp removed his shoes. His feet were blistered, wherefore he rebuked the sun and its heat and the stones on the roads, and they were dusty.

"Say from where you are, boy bach nice?" asked Ianto.

"From far enough, small male, not to want to walk another step."

"Say you where you hail from and your place of abode."

"The foxes in the fields have their holes," was the reply, "the birds of the air their nests, but I have nowhere to lay my head."

Old Ianto turned his face upon the figure on the ground, saying:

"For what you say that? Dear, dear, has not the little Big Man said, 'Ye are of more value than many sparrows'?"

"Nowhere to lay this old head," the tempter repeated through his thick lips.

"Welshman too!" exlaimed Ianto. "Not religious are your words, man. What for you don't know that you utter these vain things in the Garden of Eden? Open your eyes, and look you. Does not this river break out into four little heads? Saw you Shop Rhys as you came by? There the Creator placed Adam, and was not Adam the first sinner? Behind you is the evil tree, boy bach. See you how crooked the old trunk is! And here just is the spring that gave Eva fresh water to brew tea."

The tempter opened his heavy eyelids and said:

"You male alive, now why you are not a preacher?"

Ianto's heart rejoiced.

"Iss, indeed," he said, "this is the Garden spoken of in the Book of Words. The nice Respected Ruler of the Lord in Capel Sion says that Eva ate of the sour apples on the tree. Does not Abel Shones still pray for Eva?"

"Who is Abel Shones, whatever?" asked the tramp.

"He is the officer for Poor Relief," answered Ianto. "Wise indeed is Abel. Dear man, you should hear him praying! Asking the Big Man to help him find out wrongdoers."

"Ho, ho, and you say like that!" said the tempter.

Then Old Ianto sang, and this is what he sang:

"Iss, iss, dear man. This is the Garden of Eden. This is the beginning of the world. Goodness me, here was put breath into clay; here God gave Adam the tongue that I am speaking in now."

The song finished, the tempter said:

"Woe my poor flesh! I am tired."

"Of course, of course," said Ianto; and he raised his long, thin legs from the ground. "Do you come with me, dear stranger, and tarry a while in my house. But first put on your old shoes, for it is not seemly to go about in bare feet on the eve of the Sabbath."

Ianto took the tramp home, and he bade his daughter Dinah warm up a bowl of broth and lay it before his guest; and while the tempter ate of the broth and bread, Ianto, preparing for the Sabbath when none shall work, went to the stream and cleansed his hands and face with small gravel; and when he was returned to the house he sheared the ends of his beard.

The tempter, having eaten his meal, pulled off his shoes and lit his pipe.

"Do you ever pray, one's brother bach?" asked Ianto.

"Brother, indeed!" said Dinah.

"Hold thy chin, little Dinah," Ianto reproved her. "Brother I mean in the spirit rather than in the letter. Brother bach, do you pray steadfast?"

"What a question, dear me!" answered the tempter. "Indeed, do I not live by faith?"

Ianto placed a bunch of tobacco inside his right cheek, and the black mole thereon moved up and down and in and out in progress with it.

"Come you now," said Dinah, "speak you your name."

"Michael," said the tempter.

Ianto opened his Bible and read. Afterwards he removed the tobacco from his mouth and laid it on the table, and he reported to God with a clean mouth.

When he had risen from his knees and had shaken the stiffness out of his joints, Dinah addressed him:

"Little father, for why you are an old mule? Shame on you to bring here a dirty, bad tramp. What then will folk say? Tell you him to go about his business."

"Hush, hush, Dinah. Say you not so. 'Inasmuch as ye do unto the least of my little ones.' Michael is tired. Look you!"

The tramp had fallen asleep; a silver line of spittle ran from his lips along the stem of his pipe, dropping from the base of the bowl.

Ianto wound up his watch, and took off his clothes, and stepped over the mud floor to his bed, which stood against the nailed-down window frame.

Dinah rested her elbows on her stockinged knees, and she settled her eyes on the sleeping stranger — a muscular figure with tanned, hairy skin showing under his buttonless shirt.

Old Ianto spoke from his bed:

"Dinah, go you off to your loft now. Indulge in no evil thoughts concerning Michael. Think you no less of him, little daughter, because the Big Man has not blessed him with much."

Dinah untied the tape which held her skirt around her waist, and removed the cotton bodice which covered her loosely hanging breasts, and went up the ladder into the loft.

In the morning she baked a loaf of plank bread which, with a bowl of milk warm from the cow, she laid before the tramp. To her father she observed:

"I think that old serpent of a straggler can abide here a time, and help to do something about the place. What say you now if he set to mend the wall of the pigsty?"

The tempter fattened many days in Ianto's house. He built a new wall to the pigsty and on the inside of the door of the cowshed he contrived a trickish bolt.

On the afternoon of the second Sunday after his coming he fondled Dinah and made mischief with her, and when they had committed their sin, the woman was revengeful, and she cried to him:

"Go your way! Take to the dunghill! You lout! For sure I will shout your wickedness." She seized his head and clawed his scalp, until the tramp's hair was dyed red.

But Michael understood the ways of women, and Dinah, far from divulging what had taken place, went out in the darkness of that night, and when she had secured the door she laid with him on a little straw spread on the floor of the cow-stall.

In the ripeness of time Dinah sorely repented herself, and was much shamed; she drew in the seams of her garments, and pressed herself as butter is pressed into an overfull cask.

People remarked her, and said things one to another.

Ianto spoke to his daughter.

"Bad you were to go out of your way to tempt poor Michael. Tell you the boy bach that it's good for him to get beyond the sense of your wickedness."

Dinah acted; she said to Michael:

"Get out you of our home, the old hen! Get away off, else I'll stick this old pitchfork in your eyes."

Michael grew feared, and departed; and in a week he came back.

"Sure, dear me, now," he observed to Ianto, "you won't turn your guest into the highway. Let me rest in your house for a small period."

"Remain here as long as you like, little son," replied Ianto. "But steel your heart against the wiles of my wench."

During the month which followed Dinah employed divers methods to rid the house of Michael. On a day she said to him: "Off now, you boy bach, and buy two pounds of sugar in Shop Rhys. Take you this silver little sixpence." On another day she said to him: "Go off, now indeed to death, and change these eggs for money at Shop Rhys," and she gave him thirty eggs, each egg worth a penny. Yet on another day she said to him: "A broom I must have. Take a shilling and buy one in Shop Rhys." But Michael, to her great distress, performed these errands faithfully.

In the twilight of an afternoon Dinah was preparing Ianto's supper. Michael was sleeping in a chair under the chimney. The room was illumined by a thin light from the fire; Dinah turned around, and she beheld that Michael's feet were cloven hoofs, and that from his head there came forth two horns. In the twinkling of an eye she knew whom she had been entertaining. Hastening into the lower parlour, she placed the palms of her hands on the cover of the Bible and prayed:

"In the name of the Father, Son, and Holy Ghost, get thee behind me, Satan. Jesus bach, be with your Ruler in Capel Sion. Amen."

She re-entered the kitchen.

"Michael, man," she said, "how say you to a nice cup bach of tea?"

"Iss, indeed Dinah," answered the tramp.

Dinah lifted an empty tin pitcher.

"Dear now," she exclaimed, "what pity! There's not a drop of water. Go you and draw some."

The tramp pushed his feet into his clogs.

"Give me the old pitcher then," he said.

"Have I not need of the pitcher for milking?" Dinah said.

"I'll bring it in the bucket that is outside the pigsty," said Michael, walking towards the door.

"Don't you be dirty, boy bach," cried Dinah. "That bucket is for the pigs' wash."

Michael had moved to the threshold and was holding the door ajar. He looked along the road and saw that Abel Shones, the officer for Poor Relief, was running to the house.

He came back into the kitchen.

"What shall I fetch it in, then?" he asked. "Be you hasty now, for am I not thirsty?"

"Dear me, what a calf you are, man! Bring it in this," and Dinah gave him the cinder sifter.

Since these things happened Dinah has been blessed with second-sight and visionary power. On dark nights she goes to the well and mocks the Angel Michael, who until he performs the task that is set him, will remain upon the earth in the flesh of a tramp.

THE WOMAN WHO SOWED INIQUITY

This is the chronicle of Betti Lancoch, who was the daughter of Essec, the Essec of whom is written on his gravestone that he was possessed of two farms named Lancoch and Llanwen, that he had a name among the religious men of the Big Seat in Capel Sion. On Essec's death Betti's inheritance was Lancoch, which is the smaller of the farms; and the inheritance of her brother Joshua was Llanwen.

Until her thirtieth year Betti was a princess in Sion. Her wealth was a prize for which many intrigued and prayed; and although much gravel was thrown at her window at nights she did not give herself to anyone.

Her brother Joshua looked very keenly after her interests. He was anxious that she should marry a godly, humble man, and from the tales he told her, godly, humble men were scarce in the land. Even the character of Rhys Shop was shown in a bad light when he got to know how the white-faced, big-paunched shopkeeper one night tried to climb up the wall to the room wherein Betti slept. Joshua was married himself, and did not find much pleasure, he said, in it, and he wished to keep his sister as free and happy and pure as the Big Man had ordained she should remain. For he managed the selling of most of the produce of Lancoch and paid himself, one way or another, for his trouble.

Betti answered only too well to her brother's skilful guiding. She did not open the window of her room to any man in Capel Sion or in the place around. Now on an August day she went to Eisteddfod Castellybryn and there met Gwylim, the son of Silah and Tim, farmers in the Vale of Towy. . . . Gwylim came and courted Betti in full daylight, wherefore the men of Sion grew angry, and they called on Joshua and said to him: "Speak you to her, little Josh, for is she not your sister, man?" Joshua took counsel of God. God answered him by a dream. "Well-well, Josh bach," He said, "very terrible is this about the wench Betti. Windy is the female. Command you her to remain unwed. Moreover, not right for her to take a husband away from Capel Sion. Ach y fi! Giving her farm and pennies and silver and yellow gold to a male who worships trappings and ceremonials in the old church! Be you wrathful with her in My name." Joshua spoke these words, and more, to his sister, but Betti refused to turn from her way, for which reason Joshua and the men of Capel Sion were disquieted, and they asked God to deal according to His wisdom with this woman who wilfully strayed from the path of the religious.

Betti jerked her freckled face and snapped her fingers, and boasted in the security of her riches: "Goodness me, must then I be instructed in my doings by a pack of old hens? Sure now, I am not beholden to any in Capel Sion."

In the foolishness of her vanity she curled her yellow hair like a Jezebel, and she fashioned the front of her hair into a fringe which she wore over her forehead. Her brother Joshua came to her from Llanwen.

Betti, heedless of the cow lowing to be milked, was tying up her hair before a looking-glass.

"Woman," cried Joshua, beholding what his sister was

doing, "have you no shame? Will you bring discredit on me then?"

"Josh bach, there's good you are to call, man. Do you take this bucket of wash to the old pigs, and ask Madlen Tybach to come over and milk the cow on your way home."

"My sister Betti, for what you do not know that the wages of sin is death?" said Joshua.

"Don't you get savage, Josh. Am I not making myself look pretty for to see Gwilym's father and mother tomorrow?"

"Pretty! This too on the eve of the Sabbath! Is not a pretty woman a snare to the godly? Look you at Potiphar's wife now."

"Josh, indeed to goodness, what a talkist you are!"

"Dear me, what will Priscila say when I tell her? But then Priscila is content to stand where the little Big King has placed her — an angel ministering to me and my children."

"What do I count what Priscila thinks! Clap your lips, Josh bach."

"Don't you say wicked sayings now, Betti fach," Joshua advised her. "Speech you not that. Be you reasonable, my girl."

"So that is why you've come here?"

Joshua leaned his body against the dresser, and drew his clog from his right foot and removed the dirt that had gathered on the sole between the iron rims; and he closed his mouth so that the projecting birth-tooth in the middle of it clawed his lower lip.

"The Big Man brought my feet here, Betti fach," he remarked at last. "Listen you to me now. How would you say if I mouthed this to you: 'Betti the daughter of Essec, this bit of land is very vexatious to you. You don't get the best from it. Let me, your religious brother Joshua, trim it for you, and come you and live with us in Llanwen.'"

"Josh, indeed you are leaving Gwylim out!"

"Gwylim! You are not intent on wedding Gwylim?"

"Iss, man bach, I am. Think you I curl my hair for Rhys Shop? Think you I bought this nice white petticoat for him? Dear, there's dense."

"Mercy me, what a bad wench you are!" cried Joshua. "Have you not heard what a dissipated boy Gwylim is? Heard you not of his doings and his cheatings over cattle? Turn you away from your purpose, and act as I bid you."

"I shall wed him in front of all you say, Josh," said Betti. "Boy bach swellish is Gwylim."

"O Betti, is it a light thing to you that you take your possessions to a man who never goes to capel?"

"Little man senseless, you are eloquent! Do you think I could live for ten minutes with that old hare of your wife Priscila?"

Rhys Shop proclaimed in the Seiet that the Terrible Man's anger was like the pierce of a new pitchfork against Betti Lancoch. Joshua fell on his knees in his pew, wept, and prayed. Thus the Lord comforts His children: when Joshua arose, lo, his eyes were dry, and he turned his face upon the Big Seat, and addressed the men of the high places of Capel Sion. He said:

"Little people, I pray you now not to think too harshly of me because my sister brings this abomination upon the nice Capel. Look you mercifully upon my affliction. Priscila fach is badly cut about it. She is not here tonight. You know how it is with Priscila — how the Big Father is blessing her with another child. The Lord, little people, will administer the rod of correction on this slut who so shamelessly sows the seeds of iniquity; she will reap vanity. Stand you by me and Capel Sion: if I am wrong, sure, indeed the Big Man will send a message to Sadrach Danyrefail here."

Worshippers on their way to Capel Sion the preceding Sunday had shuddered at the sight of Betti Lancoch flaunting herself in fine garments. Rhys Shop spoke to her:

"Whisper you to me now where you are going."

"To the abode of Gwylim's people," replied Betti.

"And you say so now. There's going to be a wedding, then?"

"Iss, iss, Rhys Shop," Betti answered, and in her ostentatious pride she lifted her frock and displayed the skirt of her white petticoat.

Rhys bent himself and examined the material from which it had been made.

"Jasto!" he cried. "Tell you me now if you paid a shilling except a halfpenny a yard for this?"

Betti laughed.

"Didn't you now, Betti fach?" Rhys persisted. "Beautiful and useful is the cloth in the Shop that will do for your wedding gown. It is only half a crown a yard too. But there, don't you think any more about it. . . . Little white Jesus, forgive me for saying like this on the Sabbath. Dear me, forgetful male I was! Be with your Ruler in Sion. Amen."

"Sabbath or no Sabbath, Rhys Shop, I will not buy my wedding gown from you. To Carmarthen will I journey and get it from the grand shop of Llewellyn Shones in the market."

Rhys then walked with Bertha Daviss, to whom he spoke these words:

"Little Bertha, Abishag has gone by."

So Gwylim and Betti were married, and all in and around Lancoch having been sold and the house and the land having been rented, they went to live in the town of Carmarthen; and the house of their abode has ten stone steps in the front of it, and it is named Avon Towy because that river is the distance of a field beyond it. A year after her marriage Betti came to Manteg with her child, and she magnified brazenly the fortune of her husband. But she did not say anything of the occasions that he had come home drunk, or of the times when he had struck her with the ring end of his razor strop; nor did she show to any one the sore that was on her left breast.

The man Gwylim was foolish in his drink. He backed a bill for twenty sovereigns, and when one came to redeem it he had nothing with which to pay the price. He went to his father's house and said how this and that evil had befallen him.

"Give you the boy bach the money," said Silah to her husband Tim. "Give you him the money. This is not his fault, Little Tim. Is he not wedded to a slothful woman?"

Old Silah loved her son, and she killed for him a chicken and laid it before him. Gwylim was crafty and charged himself falsely, saying: "An old rascal am I to bring this upon you"; therefore Old Silah murmured in his hearing this lullaby:

"Pity such a concubine snared you, little Gwylim, my son bach."

Old Silah's lullaby lodged itself in Gwylim's brain; and drank he never so deep nor got he never so muddled, he remembered it always. It was as if the words were the first words he had been taught to utter.

Betti ceased to visit Manteg; she rarely went out of her house. Always she was either with child or she bore some mark of her husband's savagery; often both stopped her from going abroad. In common with the women of her race constant childbearing made her slovenly and sallow. With the birth of her fifth boy arrived her first act of humiliation: she wrote to her brother Joshua for the loan of thirty sovereigns. Joshua answered that he would lend her fifteen sovereigns provided she signed a bill of sale on Lancoch.

Betti hid away the money in a decanter.

Now it happened that on an afternoon Gwylim was very drunken, and he came to the decanter in which the money was hidden.

"Fiery Pool!" he shouted. "Where did you get this from? Oh, you've been whoring. You concubine! You slut!"

His rage was so great that he scattered the gold on the floor. Then he gathered it up and went out, and to all whom he met he groaned that a harlot had lured him and that a harlot was the mother of his children. "Did not the old mam say," he cried, "'Pity the bitch of a concubine snared you, boy bach'?"

In the morning of the day Betti opened the door of her house, and she saw that Gwylim was fallen at the foot of the stone steps, his head resting on the first step. She carried him into the house and took off his clothes and put him into bed. Before the end of the day Betti thanked God that paralysis had gripped him. Two months later a hearse took away his body to the consecrated ground where Silah and Tim will some time join him. He will rest between them.

Betti, a widow woman with five children, returned to Manteg; and in Manteg none said to her "How be things with you, Betti fach?" for is it not known that the woman who sows iniquity shall reap the fruits thereof?

Out of the wreckage she had saved enough to provide Lancoch with a poor cow, a couple of pigs, and a few hens. She tilled the soil as well as a woman without implements can till it. But stray cattle wandered into her fields because of the broken hedges, and late in the springtime a herd of cows spent a night in her garden. These cows belonged to her brother Joshua.

Betti then said to Joshua: "I might indeed as well not have touched my garden, Josh; your old cows have trampled on all my little beds."

Joshua replied: "Well-well, Betti fach, for why you do not keep your hedges in trim, then? Dear, dear, you are like the foolish virgins."

"Keep you your cows under eye," Betti answered.

"What a wicked tongue you have, Betti!" answered Joshua. "To think that we both come of the same religious father!"

Betti made no reply.

"And Betti," Joshua resumed, "the five over ten sovereigns are more than due now. Give them to me."

"Five over ten sovereigns?"

"Iss, iss. Dear me, it's a long time since I lent them to you. Much did I sacrifice for this. But I couldn't think of you going in want, Betti fach. No, no, are you not my own flesh and blood? Of course, you won't anger the Big Man by trying to cheat your brother, will you?"

"I haven't any yellow gold," Betti answered. "I don't know where to get it, unless I sell Lancoch. Indeed, I've been unlucky since I've had the place."

"Betti, for shame! Don't you blaspheme. It's the Big Man's way. And it will be sinful to sell Lancoch. Did not our father and grandfather live here?"

"What else can I do? You must have the money?"

"According to the law, Betti fach, Lancoch is mine if pay you cannot."

"Lancoch was given to me."

"For surely, Betti fach. For surely. But did you not sign the little agreement?"

"Agreement or no, Lancoch is mine."

Joshua took possession of the land around Lancoch. He put up new gates, and repaired the hedges, and divers times he drove Betti's cow out of the fields into the roadway. It was a dry summer, and water was scarce in the ditches that are alongside the roads; Betti's cow went thirsty for three days, and then she laid herself down on the moor whither she had wandered, and perished.

Joshua turned in at Lancoch.

"Little Betti," he said, "grave is the news I have for you. Priscila has promised Lancoch to Hugh the Stonemason."

"You want me to go off?"

"Glad I'll be if you go off, Betti fach."

"Where?"

"Pity now you didn't take the offer to come and live in Llanwen. I can't go back on Priscila's word to Hugh. And he'll be handy about the place. There's the money too. Josh the Small is costing me a deal now. Educating a boy to be a little preacher does take a lot of money, Betti. But I am only lending to the Big Man."

Betti broke in: "Josh, I've been a foolish woman. I rejected your counsel, and I mocked the Man of Terror. But I am humbled now, Josh bach. All the stiffness has gone out of me. And the Big Man is angry with me."

"Repent you, Betti fach, and He will forgive you."

"Little Josh, I have passed through the Pool since I wedded Gwylim. Oh, Josh," Betti cried, "deal gently with your sister nice. Turn you not me out of my home. What is the rent to you? Listen you to my plea, there's a boy bach."

"I would now, indeed, but you see Priscila has given her word —."

The infant nestling against Betti's breast touched the sore made there by the ring end of Gwylim's razor strop, and the place hurt her. She gave a cry; and with that cry there arose in her heart something of the old spirit of the woman who flaunted herself in fine vain garments on a Sabbath morning, and who laughed in the faces of the men of the Big Seat.

"Joshua," she cried, "you've stolen Lancoch from me. Dear, dear, what an old Satan you are, man! Bad you are, Joshua! Look you, so long as there's a roof over Lancoch, I will stop in the house."

"You talk like an awful woman," said Joshua. "Do you not know how you are tempting the Big Man? Be calm, you wicked spider."

Joshua knelt by his bedside that night and asked the Almighty to bring into subjection the spirit of this most stubborn of His creatures.

Betti locked the door of her house and covered the windows with boards. At the weakest point, which was in the doorway, she stood armed with a crowbar.

In the morning Joshua spoke to Hugh the Stonemason.

"I have spent the night in prayer," he said. "The Big Man has not forsaken the righteous, so whatever happens will be His doing, not ours, Hugh bach. The Lord's will be done. Go you down to Lancoch now, and take an old ladder with you and climb to the roof, and remove the tiles one by one. Be careful lest any untoward happening befall my sister Betti, for has not the white little Jesus bidden us love our enemies? Do you see, Hugh bach, that not one slate falls on the head of our sister Betti. But if one does, well-well, then, has not the Great Male promised to be on the side of His religious children?"

A JUST MAN IN SODOM

The haymakers, gathering in the hay of Sadrach Danyrefail, rested in the shadow of the hedge, eating their midday porridge and skimmed milk.

Sadrach the Small raised his voice:

"Come you now, Pedr, give us a little bit of a sermon, man. Stand you in the old cart."

"Iss, iss," said Martha, the stranger woman who ruled at Danyrefail, "do you do this thing we ask of you."

The workers raised their mouths from their wooden bowls.

"Goodness now," said Pedr, "why should I, beloved of the little Big Man, preach from a common cart when there is a pulpit in Capel Sion?"

"Oh, Pedr, Pedr," Sadrach the Small said, "do we not always say that you ought to judge us in Capel Sion? Sure there is something you can bear witness to before we go on with the old hay. Turn you your mind now, and say sayings to us."

"Think you truly I ought to be a preacher?" asked Pedr, his eyes shining with vanity. "There's happy would I be if they'd let me preach from a pulpit bach."

Sadrach the Large then addressed Pedr:

"Preach you to us for ten minutes, and I'll take a hat round for a collection. Indeed to goodness, I will now."

111

"Sadrach! Sadrach!" said Martha, "what for you make such a foolish promise? Man, man, you are as silly as Pedr. Come, little people, have you not rested long enough?"

But Pedr, open-mouthed, was standing in the cart; his large eyes looked upon the fertile land between him and Avon Bern, where grazed Sadrach's cows, the best herd in the neighbourhood, and where flourished Sadrach's corn, the most pleasing sight in all the land. Sadrach the Small threw at him a handful of horse-dung, which fell on Pedr's open lips and the never-shaved hairs that curled on his chin.

"Pedr, indeed to goodness, there's slow are you, man," remarked Sadrach the Large.

"Praying was I, Sadrach bach, for strength to speak unto this gathering."

"Sober now," said Sadrach the Large, "you must not go as far as that."

Pedr took a text and spoke to the people, whereon one turned to the other, whispering:

"Dull Pedr brays like a mule."

From where he was lying on the ground Sadrach the Small cried:

"Tell us, Pedr, man, about the vision you had the last night but one. Do you be soon."

"Woe is me!" exclaimed Pedr."The Big Man forgive me for forgetting what the little white Jesus told me."

"Come on, Pedr; come on, Pedr," cried the haymakers.

Pedr gazed on those below him.

"Boys bach nice," he said, "Jesus did speak to me about you, and He did say things of great concern about Capel Sion. My dears, do you let Pedr now say a small prayer first."

Pedr closed his eyes, and while he sang Sadrach the Small crawled forward on his belly and dug the prongs of his pitching-fork into him.

"The message! The message!" he cried. "Jasto, what a jolt-headed mare you are."

"Do you let the fool be," said Martha. "What is the matter for you, man? Come down from the old cart."

Pedr eyed the people indulgently.

"Wasn't that a fairish prayer?" he asked.

"As good as Bryn-Bevan's," was the response.

"As good as Bryn-Bevan's!" repeated Pedr.

"Iss, iss, you old owl. Deliver the message."

"Does not the least among you think he is wiser than Pedr?" he reproached them. "But am I not rich in grace? To whom did the little white Jesus come last night? He never visited even Essec. For why? Because when old Essec was dying he said wily words to his son Joshua Llanwen: 'Keep your purse full and the strings tight, and nothing will fail you.'"

"But Pedr," Sadrach the Large explained, "Essec meant these things to come after religion."

"Did he now?" said Pedr. "Dear me, there's a blockhead am I. I did not know."

"If I die, Pedr is madder than ever!" said one.

"Oh, I am wise today. Pedr is wise with the wisdom of God. Am I not among the prophets? See you, I am come after little Elijah, and Jeremiah, and Daniel. What a boy brave Dan bach was, for sure. The white Jesus said to me, 'Pedr, I look to you to save Capel Sion.'"

"If we let the dog go on blaspheming," Martha interrupted, "the revengeful Big Man will punish us with rain before half the hay is in stack."

"I am a man of God," Pedr drivelled. "Hearken you now to my voice, for do not my sayings come from Him whose mercy is as bountiful as the hay around us, and whose anger is as furious as the bull who frightened Achsah the wife of Sadrach into giving birth to Sadrach the Small on the threshold of

Danyrefail. 'The children of Capel Sion,' said the little white Jesus, 'are walking in the ways of the Bad Man.'"

"Pedr bach," said Sadrach the Large, "have you care now. Don't you, little male, trifle with the name of the Big Man."

Pedr closed his ears against the warning.

"The Big Man is angry with you," he resumed, "and His anger consumes like the fire which ate up the hay of Griffith Graig, though His mercy is as the waters of Morfa. 'Pedr bach,' said the little white Jesus, 'tell you them to turn away from their adulterous ways, for when the Lord hurteth a man He hurteth him to death. Tell you them that they are as wicked as the old blacks of Sodom.'"

Sadrach the Small flung a rake at Pedr's head.

"Now, now, that is not like the offspring of a religious father," Sadrach the Large rebuked his son. "Be you calm, my child. The temptation is great, but remember you that Pedr is not sensible in his head."

"O people," Pedr continued, "listen. Thus said the Big Man: 'Capel Sion has become as a temple of pig buyers; a woman without glory. Pedr bach, do you say to them that I will destroy their crops and rot their bones, that not one male, nor female, nor child shall rise from the grave when my little servant Gabriel blows on his old trumpet. They will abide among the filthy, creeping things of the earth.'"

Martha interposed: "Throw you the vain crow out, Sadrach, else sure something bad will hap to me and your father for harbouring him in our land."

Pedr continued: "Said the little white Jesus: 'Mind you, Pedr bach, not to forget to tell the sons of Capel Sion that they have thieved from the widow and the orphan; tell you the daughters too, Pedr bach, that they speak slander and deal lightly with the things that are holy in my sight.' There's sayings for you! What for you laugh, boys bach? Is not the Judge of the earth right?

Would you laugh at Daniel? At Elijah? Why for you laugh? You will have, dear me, to change your thinks if you will wear the White Shirts."

So Pedr assumed the mantle of a prophet. Children mocked him and stoned him, and threw clods of earth at him; men and women reviled him, inquiring of him always: "How now, Pedr, anything new from the Palace?"

He left the house where he dwelt, and went to live on the moor. There, on the brim of the stone quarry, he built a hut of mud, and the roof he covered with dry heather, and at a distance of eight feet therefrom he threw up a mound of earth which he called an altar and he dedicated it unto God.

In the hut he fasted and meditated, and by the altar he prayed continually.

The evening of the fifth day after Sadrach's hay had been stacked a heavy rain fell upon West Wales, and this rain lasted many days, destroying much of the crops. The men of the Big Seat proved the congregation, and they found that Sion was without sin, hence this deluge of rain was not a judgment upon Sion. They also gathered themselves together and prayed for deliverance.

Pedr journeyed down from the moor and waited outside the gates that admit you into Capel Sion, and as the congregation departed, he cried:

"Little people, why value you the things that perish more than the living soul?"

Sadrach Danyrefail derided him.

"A bad prophet you are indeed," he said. "What for you didn't say the rain was coming, man, so as to save all this nasty bother? Goodness me, you are a frog! There's vexed Martha is since you waggled your wild tongue in the hayfield. Prophet! Who made you judge in Capel Sion? Think you the Big Man chooses you before me and the Respected Bryn-Bevan to be

His mouthpiece?"

"Woe to you, Sadrach Danyrefail," announced Pedr. "Your dishonour makes the little angels weep."

Sadrach spat in his face.

"Dear people —" began Pedr.

"Pedr," said Sadrach, "bits of sermons now and again are all right, but when you take the name of the Big Man in vain, well-well, it is very sinful."

"My soul," exclaimed Pedr, "is as clean as the soul of Elijah."

"Hearken you now, Pedr," said Sadrach jestingly, "can you bring the dead to life? Elijah could. And, dear me, where are your sacrifices? You can't bring an old turnip to life, man."

The people pushed Pedr hither and thither. In his terror he cried loudly to God to protect his skin, but his words did not save his body from a stone nor a clod of earth.

All through that night Pedr prayed at the side of the altar he had dedicated unto the Big Father.

When Sadrach the Small fetched the cows in the morning, which was the Sabbath, he saw that the bull-calf was missing. He searched in all the fields and in many of those of his neighbours. Returning to Danyrefail, he climbed up into his father's room.

"Little father," he said, "the old bull-calf is lost, man."

"Now careless someone has been. Was the gate shut, Sadrach?"

"Indeed, iss, it was."

"The calf couldn't open the gate, boy," said Martha.

"Wise your speech," said Sadrach the Large. "Hie you and look again. But mouth you to no one your mission. Recollect that this is the Sabbath. Still, it is not sinning to look for a lost sheep on the Sabbath, but let it not be said that a bad sampler comes from Danyrefail."

That Sabbath morning Pedr hailed a man who was crossing the moor to Capel Sion.

"Man bach," he said to him, "do you hurry quickly now, and tell them in Sion to come up the mountain, because this day the Big Creator is manifesting Himself. For this hour, man bach, you are a messenger of the white little Jesus."

The man laughed the news to those with whom he fell in. He laughed it to Sadrach the Large.

"The old cuckoo must be sent to the House of the Mad," said Sadrach.

Sadrach walked as far as the gates of Capel Sion, then he turned back and went up to the moor. As he neared the hut, Pedr ran to him and threw his arm around his neck.

"Sadrach Danyrefail," he said, "there's joyous I am you've come. Sing a hymn of gladness, Sadrach Danyrefail, for today the Bad Man departs from Capel Sion."

Pedr led Sadrach to the altar, and on the top of it was the bull-calf, slowly bleeding to death.

"Son of hell!" cried Sadrach when he saw what Pedr had done. "For what do you do this with my calf which is worth great yellow gold? I'll have the law on you in half an hour, even if it is the Sabbath."

He hit out with his arm, and Pedr fell against the altar, and the blood of the calf dropped upon his face.

"Dear Sadrach," he said when he had risen to his feet, "this is the sacrifice that is going to wipe away the sins of Capel Sodom. Indeed, indeed, it is now. But, lo, the Big Man is not meanly. He is satisfied with the blood only. Look you now, I will bring back your old calf to life. The white Jesus will do this for His prophet."

Pedr removed the blood from his forehead, because it was oozing into his eyes, with a little heather, and he went and stood on the altar; and he turned his face on the dying calf and

117

stretched forth his hands.

"In the name of the little white Jesus, return you to life, little bull-calf," he said. "Jesus bach, do you bring this about for the sake of your servant's good name."

BE THIS HER MEMORIAL

Mice and rats, as it is said, frequent neither churches nor poor men's homes. The story I have to tell you about Nanni — the Nanni who was hustled on her way to prayer-meeting by the Bad Man, who saw the phantom mourners bearing away Twm Tybach's coffin, who saw the Spirit Hounds and heard their moanings two days before Isaac Penparc took wing — the story I have to tell you contradicts that theory.

Nanni was religious; and she was old. No one knew how old she was, for she said that she remembered the birth of each person that gathered in Capel Sion; she was so old that her age had ceased to concern.

She lived in the mud-walled, straw-thatched cottage on the steep road which goes up from the Garden of Eden, and ends at the tramping way that takes you into Cardigan town; if you happen to be travelling that way you may still see the roofless walls which were silent witnesses to Nanni's great sacrifice — a sacrifice surely counted unto her for righteousness, though in her search for God she fell down and worshipped at the feet of a god.

Nanni's income was three shillings and ninepence a week. That sum was allowed her by Abel Shones, the officer for Poor Relief, who each pay-day never forgot to remind the crooked, wrinkled, toothless old woman how much she owed to him and God.

"If it was not for me, little Nanni," Abel was in the habit of telling her, "you would be in the House of the Poor long ago."

At that remark Nanni would shiver and tremble.

"Dear heart," she would say in the third person, for Abel was a mighty man and the holder of a proud office, "I pray for him night and day."

Nanni spoke the truth, for she did remember Abel in her prayers. But the workhouse held for her none of the terrors it holds for her poverty-stricken sisters. Life was life anywhere, in cottage or in poorhouse, though with this difference: her liberty in the poorhouse would be so curtailed that no more would she be able to listen to the spirit-laden eloquence of the Respected Josiah Bryn-Bevan. She helped to bring Josiah into the world; she swaddled him in her own flannel petticoat; she watched him going to and coming from school; she knitted for him four pairs of strong stockings to mark his going out into the world as a farm servant; and when the boy, having obeyed the command of the Big Man, was called to minister to the congregation of Capel Sion, even Josiah's mother was not more vain than Old Nanni. Hence Nanni struggled on less than three shillings and ninepence a week, for did she not give a tenth of her income to the treasury of the Capel? Unconsciously she came to regard Josiah as greater than God: God was abstract; Josiah was real.

As Josiah played a part in Nanni's life, so did a Seller of Bibles play a minor part in the last few days of her travail. The man came to Nanni's cottage the evening of the day of the rumour that the Respected Josiah Bryn-Bevan had received a call from a wealthy sister church in Aberystwyth. Broken with grief, Nanni, the first time for many years, bent her stiffened limbs and addressed herself to the living God.

"Dear little Big Man," she prayed, "let not your son bach religious depart."

Then she recalled how good God had been to her, how He had permitted her to listen to His son's voice; and another fear struck her heart.

"Dear little Big Man," she muttered between her blackened gums, "do you now let me live to hear the boy's farewell words."

At that moment the Seller of Bibles raised the latch of the door.

"The Big Man be with this household," he said, placing his pack on Nanni's bed.

"Sit you down," said Nanni, "and rest yourself, for you must be weary."

"Man," replied the Seller of Bibles, "is never weary of well-doing."

Nanni dusted for him a chair.

"No, no; indeed now," he said; "I cannot tarry long, woman. Do you not know that I am the Big Man's messenger? Am I not honoured to take His word into the highways and byways, and has He not sent me here?"

He unstrapped his pack, and showed Nanni a gaudy volume with a clasp of brass, and containing many coloured prints; the pictures he explained at hazard: here was a tall-hatted John baptising, here a Roman-featured Christ praying in the Garden of Gethsemane, here a frock-coated Moses and the Tablets.

"A Book," said he, "which ought to be on the table of every Christian home."

"Truth you speak, little man," remarked Nanni. "What shall I say to you you are asking for it?"

"It has a price far above rubies," answered the Seller of Bibles. He turned over the leaves and read: "'The labourer is worthy of his hire.' Thus it is written. I will let you have one copy — one copy only — at cost price."

"How good you are, dear me!" exclaimed Nanni.

"This I can do," said the Seller of Bibles, "because my Master is the Big Man."

"Speak you now what the cost price is."

"A little sovereign, that is all."

"Dear, dear; the Word of the little Big Man for a sovereign!"

"Keep you the Book on your parlour table for a week. Maybe others who are thirsty will see it."

Then the Seller of Bibles sang a prayer; and he departed.

Before the week was over the Respected Josiah Bryn-Bevan announced from his pulpit that in the call he had discerned the voice of God bidding him go forth into the vineyard.

Nanni went home and prayed to the merciful God:

"Dear little Big Man, spare me to listen to the farewell sermon of your saint."

Nanni informed the Seller of Bibles that she would buy the Book, and she asked him to take it away with him and have written inside it an inscription to the effect that it was a gift from the least worthy of his flock to the Respected Josiah Bryn-Bevan, D.D., and she requested him to bring it back to her on the eve of the minister's farewell sermon.

She then hammered hobnails into the soles of her boots, so as to render them more durable for tramping to such capels as Bryn-Bevan happened to be preaching in. Her absences from home became a byword, occurring as they did in the haymaking season. Her labour was wanted in the fields. It was the property of the community, the community which paid her three shillings and ninepence a week.

One night Sadrach Danyrefail called at her cottage to commandeer her services for the next day. His crop had been on the ground for a fortnight, and now that there was a prospect of fair weather he was anxious to gather it in. Sadrach was going to say hard things to Nanni, but the appearance of the gleaming-eyed creature that drew back the bolts of the door frightened him and tied his tongue. He was glad that the old woman did not invite him inside, for from within there issued an abominable smell as might have come from the boiler of the witch who one time lived on the moor. In the morning he saw Nanni trudging towards a distant capel where the Respected Josiah Bryn-Bevan was delivering a sermon in the evening. She looked less bent and not so shrivelled up as she did the night before. Clearly, sleep had given her fresh vitality.

Two Sabbaths before the farewell sermon was to be preached Nanni came to Capel Sion with an ugly sore at the side of her mouth; repulsive matter oozed slowly from it, forming into a head, and then coursing thickly down her chin on to the shoulder of her black cape, where it glistened among the beads. On occasions her lips tightened, and she swished a hand angrily across her face.

"Old Nanni," folk remarked while discussing her over their dinner-tables, "is getting as dirty as an old sow."

During the week two more sores appeared; the next Sabbath Nanni had a strip of calico drawn over her face.

Early on the eve of the farewell Sabbath the Seller of Bibles arrived with the Book, and Nanni gave him a sovereign in small money. She packed it up reverently, and betook herself to Sadrach Danyrefail to ask him to make the presentation.

At the end of his sermon the Respected Josiah Bryn-Bevan made reference to the giver of the Bible, and grieved that she was not in the Capel. He dwelt on her sacrifice. Here was a Book to be treasured, and he could think of no one who would treasure it better than Sadrach Danyrefail, to whom he would hand it in recognition of his work in the School of the Sabbath.

In the morning the Respected Josiah Bryn-Bevan, making a tour of his congregation, bethought himself of Nanni. The thought came to him on leaving Danyrefail, the distance betwixt which and Nanni's cottage is two fields. He opened the door and called out:

"Nanni."

None answered.

He entered the room. Nanni was on the floor.

"Nanni, Nanni!" he said. "Why for you do not reply to me? Am I not your shepherd?"

There was no movement from Nanni. Mishtir Bryn-Bevan went on his knees and peered at her. Her hands were clasped tightly together, as though guarding some great treasure. The minister raised himself and prised them apart with the ferrule of his walking-stick. A roasted rat revealed itself. Mishtir Bryn-Bevan stood for several moments spellbound and silent; and in the stillness the rats crept boldly out of their hiding places and resumed their attack on Nanni's face. The minister, startled and horrified, fled from the house of sacrifice.

THE REDEEMER

Adam the son of Bern-Davydd — Bern-Davydd being the Ruler of Capel Sion before the day of Bryn-Bevan — was walking along the Road of the Romans, the narrow way that begins at the forehead of the School and disappears in the heather of the moor. His companion was Lissi, the servant of Ellen the Weaver's Widow.

Midway there is a breach in the hedge, wherein, on a big stone, Adam and Lissi rested, and while they rested Joshua Llanwen came upon them. Joshua said: "Say you are Adam the son of Bern-Davydd, boy, and the wench Lissi?"

"Iss, iss, little Adam am I."

"Now what for you mean to be here in the dark?" said Joshua.

Adam arose to his feet and answered:

"Goodness me, Josh bach, are we not going home?"

"What a big iob you are, you bull-calf!" Joshua shouted. "Why for you are an old cow, man? The other road is to the Shepherd's Abode. Have I not pledged that this is not to happen?"

He clenched his hand and thrust out the joint of his second finger, and therewith dealt Adam three blows on the face. Adam fell into the hedge, and while he nursed his sores he moaned:

"Dear Josh bach, why then you are so hasty, man? Sure now you have cut my nice face!"

Joshua, ignoring the plaint, turned upon Lissi:

"Back you hie, you brazen slut! Turn your wicked eyes and foul heart to Ellen's loom-shed. You sow, walk you off in front of me."

Lissie obeyed; as she moved towards the School Joshua raised his foot and kicked her.

Presently Adam scrambled over the hedge and across pastureland and gorse hurried to his father's house. This he did because he was feared of meeting Joshua on the road.

Bern-Davydd heard the sound of the gate opening, whereupon he lifted his eyes to his son Lamech and to Lamech's wife Puah, and said:

"Don't you muchly catechise Adam. Is not Joshua an eager counsellor? Perhaps his sayings have brought reason into the boy's heart. Make pretence you are reading your old books."

Thus, when Adam came into the room, no face was raised to him, nor voice said to him: "Dear me now, who has come for fresh garments this day? Much silver the tailor is gathering," or "Well-well, little Adam, now that you've come, our religious father will thank the Big Father for the mercies of the hour, and we'll go to bed," this latter being the fashion the household of Bern-Davydd had of spending the last wakeful moments of the eve of the Sabbath. The transparent china lamp on the tinsel-draped mantelpiece lit up the group on the hearth: Bern-Davydd, a loosely woven rope of whitish hair like a coil of sheep's wool which has been caught in a barbed wire, and exposed many days to the weather, extending from ear to ear; Lamech, the ball of his small nose glittering against swarthy skin and bushy black beard and moustache: Puah, her feet resting on the fender, and the tuft of red hair on the right side of her mouth shivering like boar's hairs between the fingers of an ancient cobbler as she turned over the leaves of the book she was not reading.

Adam unravelled his leather boot-laces, speaking the meanwhile:

"Dear folk, a sober thing has happened to me this night. Seven times did Joshua Llanwen beat my face. Puah, look you at me now. Touch my hand and speak to them how it trembles."

Puah showed kindness to him and did as he had asked her.

"Iss, indeed," she said, "there's blood on your cheeks, Adam bach."

"What foolish man Josh is! Has he not opened the gash I did with the razor?"

Lamech chided from his chair:

"Brother Adam, heard you never of the speech of the Man of Terror, saying, 'Vengeance is mine'?"

"Little Lamech, did not Joshua strike me seven times on my nice chin?"

"Adam, the son of Bern-Davydd, listen you to me, man. Is it not written, 'Hard is the way of the transgressor'?"

The Respected Bern-Davydd said:

"Let me speak to the Big Man."

A period of twelve years divided these two sons of Bern-Davydd, the years of Lamech, the elder, being fifty-two. At the age of forty-eight Lamech wedded Puah the widow of John Shop Morfa, at whose death she inherited the shop, many book debts, and much gold; and now, the harvest of debts having been gathered in and the shop sold, Lamech received a call to preach the Word, and was spending a little time in the Shepherd's Abode before entering College Carmarthen.

But Adam the younger son was imbued with little understanding; he had never risen above working in Shop Pugh Tailor. Six months before this night he had desired Lissi, the squint-eyed girl that Ellen the Weaver's widow got from

Castellybryn Poorhouse. He had sent her a letter, which Samson Post spoke in the public places. Thereafter Lissi waited for Adam every night outside Shop Pugh Tailor.

His doings came to the ears of Lamech and Puah, who shook their heads dismally, the wife saying to her husband:

"Vile is Adam to covet the flesh of a poorhouse brat."

"Doleful is my heart and anxious," said Lamech.

"Go you and tell our father about this madness," observed Puah.

Lamech opened his Bible for spiritual guidance; he read aloud these words: "Ye shall bring down my grey hairs with sorrow to the grave."

"Throw you your light of wisdom on the speech, Lamech," said Puah.

"The Big Man means that it's better for others to tell our father. Adam may plead that what we say is not true, and we will be rebuked. Let some cunning one go and bear witness."

Puah tied her wide bonnet strings under her chin, and drew on her feet her elastic-side boots, and went to Llanwen and told Joshua to go and inform her father-in-law of the wickedness of Adam.

"For why he is so blind, Respected Bern-Davydd?" said Joshua. "And he our ruler too! If he cannot perceive the enemy in his own household, how expect he to find him among the congregation? One of his own lambs goes astray."

"Joshua Llanwen, speak you plain to me now."

"Is not that ram of an Adam courting Lissi, the poorhouse bitch that works at Ellen's loom? The pig that cackles his son to the Pool! The bellows that blows him into the arms of Satan! Why do Adam and her go each night on the Road of the Romans? Bern-Davydd, this is no light matter to him."

"Woe is me!" cried Bern-Davydd. "A sinner from my loins! . . . This must end. Joshua Llanwen, be you another Paul. Keep watch over my son on the Road of the Romans. Stay in hiding, and if you see anything wrong, show yourself, and counsel him, and drive the evil spirit out of him."

So Adam came home with blood on his chin, hence Bern-Davydd knew that Joshua Llanwen had performed his services faithfully; and on many occasions Joshua chastised Adam with his tongue, and his fists, and with the oaken club he employed to break in horses. Yet Adam would not leave off courting Lissi.

One night Bern-Davydd and his son Lamech spoke to Adam of their grief. Bern-Davydd said: "Uncomfortable you make us. There's little you show yourself in the sight of Capel Sion."

"Mouth you to us now," said Lamech, "that you will let the bad wench be."

"Iss, say you like that," said Puah. "Think you the Big Man has chosen such as Lissi to be a Bern-Davydd?"

"Little people," answered Adam, "shortsighted you be then. Expect you, Lamech, the Big Father to perform a miracle with Puah as He did with Sara? Will she conceive and bear for you a child? Puah has passed her fruitfulness, and am I not the hope of the Bern-Davydds?"

"But, dull Adam bach," said Puah, "why do you go low for a female? Mercy me! Lissi a Bern-Davydd! Repent you now, and be a goldy boy."

Bern-Davydd's heart hardened against his stubborn son, and the colour of his face became that of the sun-dried walls of the quarry on the moor; and he informed God of a just punishment for those who rebel.

Soon people began to whisper that before long Adam would be a father; the whisper rose into a shout, and it was cried on the tramping way, and even at the gates of Capel Sion. Bern-Davydd and Lamech heard it, and they trembled. The father proclaimed from the pulpit:

"I have searched my soul for some sin that, unbeknown to myself, I might have committed. Did I find any? No, indeed to goodness, now, I didn't. Yet the Big Man's hand is hard on the innocent. My clean heart is bowed with shame. Why does the Big Father punish His child so? Last night I said to Him: 'Lead me, big Jehovah bach.' Perhaps, dear me, Adam has inherited the vanity of his mother Silah. Pray for her, you boys bach religious of the Lord."

Three mournful days passed, then Bern-Davydd said to Lamech:

"Go down and examine the dirty clod. Look you for signs if she is indeed with child. The wench may be crafty in the manner of her clothes. And, little saintly son, get you her to admit that others have been with her."

Puah interrupted: "I will go with Lamech, for I am a woman, and do I not understand the signs?"

Lissi was at her loom when Lamech and Puah came into the shed.

"Hai, the dirty wench! Walk here and stand forth, you hussy," cried Lamech.

Lissi rose from her loom and came to Lamech and his wife, and as she got near they observed that the front of the girl's petticoat hung high and away from her clogs and grey stockings.

"Ach y fi! Take," said Puah, "the stuffing away from your belly."

"Indeed me," answered Lissi, "not stuffing is here for surely. Full is my skin."

"O you Jezebel!" Puah cried. "Tell me, you ugly creature, how with your squint you tempted Adam bach."

"Speak of the others who have been bad with you," said Lamech.

Lissi, her mouth expressing an unintelligible grin, her large fingers twisting and untwisting a length of yarn, stood before them mute as a sheep in the hands of the shearer.

"Indeed to goodness now," Puah went on, "imagine you that Adam will marry you?"

The girl whined: "He'll have to. Ellen says I can petty sessions him if he refuses."

"For sure now, Lissi, Adam is not the father of the child," Puah said.

"What for you talk," Lissi replied, her spirit rising, "for was he not bad with me the night Josiah Llanwen's bull-calf perished?"

"Iss, Lissi fach," said Puah, "Josh Llanwen did this and that to your flesh."

"No, indeed, he didn't."

"Lissi, Lissi, that night on the Road of the Romans, now. . . . Iss, iss, of course he was. Did he not put you on the old stone?"

"No, no."

"Josh has repented," Puah said. "Does he not say, 'I am the father of Lissi's child'?"

"Sure me, Joshua is the father," said Lamech. "His poor old flesh couldn't withstand the temptation. But Capel Sion won't be hard on you, Lissi, nor on Josh. Isn't he the father, little daughter fach?"

"For sure, no," answered Lissi. "Josh Llanwen is important in Sion. Is not Priscila his wife? The father of the child is Adam. Did not Ellen peep into the shed?"

"Be you religious, Lissi," Puah urged. "Do you admit to Josh. If you die in childbirth there's glad you'll be that you won't cross the Jordan with a lie in your head."

"Great will be your reward," Lamech added. "You can say to the Large Spirit, 'I am the truth.'"

"But Joshua has not been bad with me," Lissi persisted.

After the result of this conversation had been reported to Bern-Davydd, Puah spoke to her father-in-law. Her words pleased him, and he marvelled at her skill and prudence.

Dusk having fallen, Puah went over pasture and gorse to the Road of the Romans. In the breach in the hedge she hid behind the stone, and she remained there until Adam and Lissi came by; and when she heard the girl coming back alone she placed over herself a bed sheet, and thus covered she stood in the middle of the way. Lissi saw her thus arrayed, and she was very frightened. She threw off her clogs and ran. Before she reached the forehead of the School she was overtaken by unfamiliar pains. . . . The child she delivered — a man child — was dead, and from her travail Lissi passed into madness.

AS IT IS WRITTEN

Samson Post placed his arms on the gate of the close of Penyrallt, and cried loudly:

"Mali! Mali! Be you quick and come, woman. Have I not a letter from your son Dan? Mali fach, do you haste now. Woe me, there's provoking you are to keep the post waiting!"

From the inside of the pigsty Mali answered:

"What old hurry you are in, man! Do you wait one little minute and I'll be with you."

Mali stooped her legs because she was too fat to bend the middle of her body, and came forth out of the pigsty, and while she scraped off the refuse from off the sides of her clogs, she called out:

"A writing from Dan, Samson bach?"

"Iss, iss," answered Samson, "take you the old letter."

"Goodness now, whatever does the boy say then? Little Samson, don't you stand there like dolted idiot. Speak Dan Bach's words."

"Dan says he is coming home for a small holiday," said Samson, opening the envelope. "And he is bringing a maid with him."

"What for you say jokes, man! Be serious and truthful."

"Mali the daughter of Mati and the wife of Shaci, truthful

I am, indeed, dear me."

"Peer at the letter now, Samson bach, and interpret it to me without deceit," said Mali.

"Woman alive, not joking am I. Do I not speech that Dan and his maid will be home on the third day then?"

"Dan bach and his maid! Serious now? Who may she be? Samson, Samson, there's shut up you are. Tell her name, man?"

"Curious was Mati your old mother, and curious you are, Mali. But wait a bit now while I have another peep at the old letter. . . . Dear, where is she? Here she is. Alice Wite — that's her name, Mali. Miss Wite."

"That's vile English," said Mali.

"English, little Mali."

"Doesn't the boy say how much yellow gold she possesses?"

"No-no, woman."

"Then she hasn't got any. Wite, indeed! There's a bad concubine! For what then Dan doesn't throw gravel at the window of some tidy wench who can speak his native tongue!"

Mali threw her voice across the close and into the corner of the field which is behind the barn where Shaci her husband was thatching his hay.

"Shaci, man! Are you deaf then, for sure! Why you do not listen? Come you here at once."

Shaci came down to the earth and walked to the gate slowly, for though he was not old, he stooped because of much earth toil.

When he was within twenty paces of her, Mali called to him:

"Samson the Post does say that Dan bach is coming home on the third day with an old bitch of an English maid. A cow as poor as a church mouse, I wager."

"Iss, iss, Shaci bach," said Samson the Post, "what talk there is in Shop Rhys about Dan! The religious Respected Bryn-Bevan was there, and did he not say that the abodes of the old

English are refreshment places on the way to the Pool? Grand indeed he spoke. Like a sermon."

"Whatever is the matter with the boy?" said Shaci. "Little Samson, read you writing of the letter now to me."

"Shaci! Shaci!" Samson admonished him. "Inconsiderate you are, man. Know you not that I am the post? Has there not been a letter in my bag for three days for the owl of a Schoolin' telling him the day of Sara's funeral?"

Mali was sorrowful that her son Dan was to be charged with this fault, and she said to her husband:

"Shaci bach, here's disgrace. Put your old head into the words that Dan has written."

But Samson the Post had taken away the letter.

"Full of wrath am I," said Shaci.

"Heard you what the old Satan said about the Respected Bryn-Bevan?"

"Iss, iss."

"This thing must not come to pass. How shall we hold up our heads in Capel Sion if Dan weds an old foreign leech?"

Shaci went out, and while he was labouring he thought out a device and he came into the house to take counsel of his wife. This is what he said to Mali:

"Hearken to my speech, now, Mali fach. I will, dear me, go to Mistress Morgan Post and ask her to send a little telegram to Dan saying: 'Remember Capel Sion, Dan bach.'"

"Why speak so wasteful?" Mali replied. "Six red pennies old telegrams cost, and is not Mistress Morgan meanly? She won't take a small penny off the price."

"True-true. Iss, indeed."

Night came on, and Shaci read the words with which Moses praised the Big Man for the deliverance of the children of Israel from the hands of the Egyptians.

But Mali did not hear anything of that which Shaci said

under the open chimney or that which he read by the light of the tallow candle. She felt shame for Dan, her son, whose name would be denounced from the pulpit and spoken with scorn by the congregation, and she remembered his deeds, first and last. Dear people, why was it destined for Dan to trespass in the eyes of Sion? Heart alive, are not the evil ways of the English known far and wide? And their helpless wastefulness? Look you at Owen, the son of Antony. Owen was in a grand shop draper in Swansea. He took to himself as wife a daughter of the English, and she kept a house for lodgers. Goodness me, is it not engraved on Owen's tombstone in the Old Burial Ground in Capel Sion that he left only one hundred yellow sovereigns? Does not Antony lament to this day that Owen bach would have left half a hundred more yellow sovereigns if he had wedded a Welsh maid? Little Big Man, for why has not a Welsh maid, with a bit of land in her own name, found favour with Dan bach? There's sad it is.

Shaci closed his Bible.

"Pray will I now, Mali fach," he said, "for Dan."

"What for you pray, Shaci," answered Mali, "and do nothing? Say now we got Sadrach Danyrefail to come and speak to the boy."

"Good that would be."

"And Joshua Llanwen."

"He too is a man of God."

Shaci went to Llanwen and spoke to Joshua by the ditch under the house.

"Mali is wanting you to speak wise words to Dan," he said.

"Dan's sins have reached my ears," said Joshua. "By and by I will say phrases to the dear Big Man, and the words of the Terrible One will scorch your son Dan."

Shaci then went across the fields (for this horrid thing made him fearsome of showing his face to his neighbours, lest they should reproach him) to Danyrefail.

"Shaci! Shaci! Go you and wash your dirty old heart," cried Martha to him. "Unworthy you are."

"Now-now, humble is my carcase," replied Shaci.

"But are you humble before the Almighty?" cried Martha the stranger woman of Danyrefail. "Drato, go on your dirty knees, old boy ugly."

"There's no more spirit left in me, little Martha," said Shaci. "Do you now in the godliness of your heart say to Sadrach the Large that I seek his instruction."

Sadrach took Shaci aside to speak to him quietly.

"Sure, little Shaci," he ended, "come I will to prove this foreign hussy with hard questions."

So Shaci's heart was lightened, and he walked home over the tramping road; and though many asked him this and thus, he saw none mocking him to his face.

When he got home Mali was moaning her grief to Bertha Daviss, and Rhys Shop, and Sali the wife of Old Shemmi.

"For why does poor Dan bach want to bring home a bad woman from the English?" she said. "Alice Wite. There's a nasty wench! The cunning serpent to lure away my boy bach. And I dare wager she is as poor as Old Nanni's rats."

Rhys Shop opened his lips and made utterance:

"Vain are the English women who work in these shops. Did not Tom Hughes, the traveller, say they are all wasteful?"

"And, little Rhys," Bertha Daviss said, "did he not say they are barren? Sober! Sober!"

"Recollect you the female maid who stayed with Wynne the vicar?" said Sali the wife of Old Shemmi. "Goodness, what an old girl she was, for sure! She washed her flesh on the Sabbath in Avon Bern."

"Say not like that," Rhys Shop interrupted.

"Iss, she did. Did not word of her doings reach Shemmi's

ears, and did he not hide himself behind Sadrach's hedge to see the shameless woman for himself? And she used to take her old pagan dog for walks over the fields on the afternoons of the Sabbath."

"Dear people," said Rhys Shop, "have we not much to be thankful for to the Big Man?"

"Indeed, iss," said Bertha Daviss.

"The little white Jesus will do me badly if I give the bitch a bed in my house," said Mali.

"Tell you me now what you are going to do with her?" asked Sali the wife of Shemmi.

"Sadrach the Large and Joshua Llanwen will prove her," answered Shaci.

"Proper indeed to ask the Respected Bryn-Bevan to speak to her also," said Bertha. "Go you off, the two of you together, and speak to him."

Mali followed closely behind Shaci, and she was weeping the whole of the way, and her grief was so much that she spoke to none of the people who asked of her: "Mali fach, what for you weep, woman nice?"

"Come into the cowshed, sinners bach," said the Respected Bryn-Bevan; "the mistress has been washing the flags. Ho, iss, the hand of the Lord is hard upon you this day."

"Iss, Respected bach," said Shaci.

"This thing, Shaci, does not please me. Samson Post came to me for guidance, and we agreed that Wite is not a Welsh word. Ho, Shaci, no one in the Book of Words is named Wite."

"Mishtir Bryn-Bevan!"

"Not one, indeed."

"Awful," said Shaci.

"Sinful," said the minister.

"Do him come in the neighbourhood of five in the afternoon and say a speech," said Mali. "Thankful will we be if he do this great deed."

"Sure me, I'll come, Shaci. Has not the Big Man called me to judge over Sion? I'll talk fair to the wench, and if she bears herself without modesty in my presence then I will deal mightily with her."

Now in the order of their importance these are they that went up to Penyrallt the day that Dan brought home a daughter of the English: the Respected Bryn-Bevan, Sadrach the Large, Joshua Llanwen, Rhys Shop, Sali the wife of Old Shemmi, Bertha Daviss.

The Respected Bryn-Bevan sat at the round table in the parlour, and the door of the parlour was kept open so that his voice reached the others who sat in the kitchen.

Mishtir Bryn-Bevan's reading of the seventh chapter of Proverbs ended when Shaci brought his horse and cart into the close.

Rhys Shop rose to his feet and moved towards the outer door.

Mishtir Bryn-Bevan spoke wrathfully.

"Rhys Shop," he cried, "an old black you are to forget that I am here!"

The minister strode through the kitchen: the people remarked the dignity of his stride and marvelled.

Shaci approached him, shaking his head, and saying,

"The old wench does not speak Welsh."

Mishtir Bryn-Bevan stood on the threshold, his feet far from each other; and he stretched forth his right arm, and his hand was covered in black kid, and he cried:

"Halt, you female woman. Why you come here to spoil this godly house? Dan who is in a shop draper in Llanelly and who is the son of Mali and Shaci, why must you tempt the Big Man to anger, boy? Mournful is your dirt. Pack you the woman about her business; let her walk in shame back to her own people."

The woman's lips quivered, and she was neither young nor pretty.

Mali came down to her.

"Our little daughter," she said, "dost her come here to take our son bach away from us now? Let her him be. Shaci will take her back to Castellybryn in the old cart."

The woman whom Dan had brought home could not answer a word, because she did not know the meaning of the words Mali had spoken. Dan was about to open his lips, when Sadrach addressed the minister.

"Mishtir Bryn-Bevan," he said, "you are a great scholar. Do you inquire of the fool if she can milk a cow."

"Iss," said Joshua Llanwen, "and if she can clean a stable."

"And tell the rat of a bitch," shouted Mali, "that Dan won't get a red penny piece after us."

"But, man fach," Dan broke in, "what does that matter? Is not Alice the owner of a nice shop draper?"

Mali now went to Dan, and she called him her own boy bach, and the son of his mother; and she took Dan and his maid into the parlour, and closed the door on them.

Returning to the congregation, she delivered to them this speech:

"There's good you were to come. Dan's maid, dear me, has travelled a long distance this day. Weary she is. Gracious now, isn't she tidy? English she may be, but has not the Big Man told us to love our enemies? Shop Draper! There's wealth for you. Rhys, come you up on a night and speak to her."

To her husband Shaci she said:

"Go you off away down to the Shop and get white flour. I will make a little lot of pancakes for Dan's maid. Be you fleet of foot."

§A BUNDLE OF LIFE

Word reached Jos Gernos — Gernos is on the brink of the ascent into the sea of Morfa — that the inheritance of Leisa the only child of Nansi and Silas Penlon was to be nearly one hundred acres of land and all the gold that had been gathered by Silas. After deliberating on this for a day, Jos said to his mother that he was going forth to compromise Leisa; he strapped whipcord leggings over his legs, and saddled his pony, and rode out to Penlon; but Leisa did not respond to the small stones he threw at her window. Jos went back to Gernos, and in the morning he wrote a letter to Leisa, and he sent it by the hand of Samson Post, and he waited for an answer until after the Sabbath, but none came. Jos refused to give over his design on Leisa's inheritance, because he had much need of money: on the fourth night Leisa took out the paper that filled a broken pane in the window and cried to him:

"Say from where you are?"

"Boy bach from Gernos am I," said Jos.

"Indeed, boy bach, all right; is not the old ladder in the cowhouse?"

Three weeks expired and on a day Jos rode away from Penlon before sunrise, and returned when Nansi was putting the milk into the separator.

"Little Jos," she said, "for why he is so early?"

"Woman, woman," replied Jos, "now-now, do I not bring with me a ring for wedding? Look you, indeed."

Nansi's face was bound with bands of flannel, which day and night wear had made hard, and which stood on her cheeks in the manner of a horse's bonnet. Her upper lip was broken into a gap that let out a little blood while she spoke, and this blood she licked away with her tongue.

"What did he give for the old ring?" she asked. "A crown, shall I say?"

Jos showed his narrow teeth. "A yellow sovereign all but a crown," he answered. "If I die, go she and speak to Peter Shop Watches in Castellybryn."

"Little Jos Gernos," said Nansi, "there's wasteful he is. Why he now go to Betti the widow of Shim, and say to her: 'Betti fach, lend me your old ring for to wed Leisa the daughter of Silas Penlon. In want you are, Betti, and I will reward you with buttermilk.'"

Jos shifted a foot, and placed it near the milk that had escaped and had formed into a small pool in a hollow in the earthen floor.

"Jos, Jos, what a frog he is!" Nansi admonished him. "Don't he move his foot now till I have scooped the precious milk up into a clean pan."

Having done this, Nansi called: "Silas now, Jos Gernos is here with his old ring."

Silas, straightway from his bed and clad in flannel drawers and soleless stockings, entered the zinc-roofed dairy.

"Did he go to the fair?" he asked Jos.

"Iss, iss, little man."

"How was the prices now?"

"Sober, little man. Sober bad."

"Did he sell his colt? Dewi says he had one to sell."

"What Dewi says is the truth."

"What did the old colt bring?"

"Little man, I didn't sell."

Jos placed a wooden bowl into the milk and drank therefrom.

"Well, Silas Penlon," he observed, "here is the costly ring. Has he matter to say why Leisa should not share my bed?"

"Not that I know of, Jos Gernos. But do he marry from Gernos, for Nansi here has not time to see to these things."

After they had spoken about this which was going to happen, and Jos had gone his way, Nansi said these words in praise of Jos.

"Old Jos is very tidy."

Silas clothed himself and went to the house of Bertha Daviss, and Bertha cut three carrots into small pieces and fried them for him, and also brewed tea for him. Silas seldom ate at home; had not Nansi and Leisa and his manservant Dewi enough to do with the care of ten cows and ten pigs and three horses without wasting time in the preparation of food? Thus he journeyed from cottage to cottage, at each cottage eating fried carrots and drinking tea. That was the period when his riches made him a power in the land, and when housewives pandered to him because of his riches.

"Old Jos Gernos is talking about taking Leisa to his bed," said Silas.

"What you call, man bach? But large has been the courting in Penlon," said Bertha.

Silas took out of the frying-pan as much of the carrots as would fill his mouth.

"Glad I'll be to see her going," he said. "She's lately taken to attending the foolish singing class in Capel Sion. And she changes her garments to go there."

"And you say that, little Silas! Have you killed your hay yet?"

"Dewi and Nansi are killing today."

Silas ate and drank, and departed.

Noontide he was sitting on the gate of the field in which Nansi and Dewi were mowing his hay. There came to him a stalwart man named Abram Bowen, who then was the chief singing man in Capel Sion.

"Dear now, very good crop of hay you've got, man," said Abram Bowen. "Silas bach, is this not a credit to you?"

Nansi and Dewi were approaching the gate, making great curves with their scythes. Nansi paused and looked at the men.

"Nansi, you silly cow," cried Silas, "what for you wait? Dewi will cut off your little legs if you don't go faster. Do you hurry now, for the night cometh."

"Happy I am to hear you saying from the Book of Words," said Abram Bowen. "Dear, dear, am I not always holding you up as a religious example in the School of Sabbath? . . . . There's old talk that Leisa is going to Gernos?"

"So they say, Abram. So they say."

"Pity now she's leaving the singing class. She mustn't go before the party bach tries at Eisteddfod Morfa."

"Well-well, mouth you to the wench herself about that."

. . . . .

That night Leisa heard the sound of gravel falling on the pane of her window. Through the hole in the pane she called out:

"You blockhead of a tadpole, is not the old ladder by the pigsty?"

Abram Bowen fetched the ladder and climbed into Leisa's room.

"Bad jasto!" Leisa exclaimed, when she knew who her visitor was. "For why you was not Jos Gernos! Abram Bowen, you frightened me, man, you did."

A tallow candle burnt on the chair, and Leisa was on one side of the bed and Abram was on the other side.

"Put on your petticoats now," said Abram. "Not religious that I eye any of your naked flesh bach. But don't do that, Leisa; I'll blow on the old candle. How speak you then about Eisteddfod Morfa?"

. . . . .

At the end of the tenth day, when Nansi was pitching the last load of hay on to the stack, Jos Gernos came to the close of Penlon and he took his pony into a field and said to him: "Go you now, beast bach, and eat a little grass." Having done that he came into the barnyard and censured Nansi severely:

"Evil Nansi, for what she has not heard about her daughter Leisa?"

"Sober, sober, what's this Jos bach Gernos would say to me now?"

"Leisa won't wed me! And did not the old ring cost me a whole yellow sovereign? As I live! Go you and ask Peter Shop Watches."

Nansi, not ceasing in her labour, cried:

"Silas, do you come and converse with Jos bach Gernos."

Silas was counting up the irregular lines, each line representing a load of hay, which he had scratched on the door of the stable.

"Well, Jos Gernos?" asked Silas.

"Leisa says she won't come to Gernos."

"Man, man!"

"Iss, the female is wedding Abram Bowen. Try he to make her sense better, little Silas."

Thrice Silas spat on the ground, for his mind was grief-stricken.

"Nansi," he said, "Leisa is going against her father."

"So Jos Gernos does say."

"You have been a bad mother to the wench," Silas shouted. "What for you have not looked after her, you old ram?"

Nansi came out of the cart, now that it was empty, and raked together the small hay that lay scattered on the ground, and while she was doing this she said:

"Silas bach, speak you not harshly to me now. Am I not always out in the fields tending the animals and seeing to the crops? Your little place needs a lot of watching."

Silas took his stick, and went out into the high roads groaning.

He came upon Abram Bowen sitting on a log of wood outside his mother's house; marking up the hymn-tunes for the Sabbath's services, and humming them over.

"Abram," said Silas, "what's this do I hear about you?"

"Speak on, little Silas."

"Sure now, you don't speech that Leisa is to wed you?"

"Dear me, iss."

"Don't you be hard of heart, Abram bach," said Silas. "Say you that people are voicing lying stories."

"Shameful you talk, Silas Penlon," Abram said. "Angry is the Big Man against you."

"Has she not laid with Jos Gernos? Has not the boy bought a ring for wedding?"

Abram Bowen sang:

"O Silas Penlon, why you are not religious? Is it for you to throw stones? Old male you are, Silas, indeed to goodness, and the time is shortly coming for you to be screwed down in your coffin."

"Abram Bowen," Silas urged, "do you listen to reason now, there's a nice, godly little boy bach."

"Silas Penlon," answered Abram, "I say unto you, sinner, that you will go down on your knees and thank the Big Man that I came to Penlon. Dear me, there's dirty the place is, man. I will plough your land and sow seeds, and the land will be yellow with corn."

"In the name of the Big Man," cried Silas, "you shall not come to Penlan," and he was going to hit Abram with his stick.

Abram stayed Silas's arm, saying: "Where is that stick with you?" When he had taken the stick away from him, he said: "Wicked you are, man. Pray to the Big Man for a little grace."

Silas moaned, for he knew that Abram Bowen was a man of nothing, and his tears mixed with the tobacco spittle that dribbled from each corner of his mouth and formed curves around his chin, and stained the tannish fringe of hair thereon.

Leisa wedded Abram Bowen, and in a set time she gave birth to a child, whom Abram named Jos, saying: "This is Leisa's bundle of sin."

Abram made fruitful the starving soil of Penlon; and he caused a brick flooring to be put in the dairy, and trained Leisa to wash her hands before separating milk and before making butter.

And as Abram grew in strength and regard, so the spirit of Silas forsook him. His name was derided at wheresoever it was said, and people sneered at him in his presence. None fried carrots nor brewed tea for him any more. He submitted unto the new King.

Once he said to Bertha Daviss:

"Dammo, boy of Satan is Abram."

Whereupon Bertha went to Penlon and said to Abram:

"Terrible indeed to goodness is Silas's tongue about you, little Abram."

Abram ordered Nansi to give Bertha a pat of butter, and then hurried to the tramping road. He met Silas outside Shop Rhys, and in the eye of the village he thrashed the blasphemy out of him. After that there was no more spirit left in Silas.

In their day Silas and Nansi had saved eighty sovereigns, and when Abram had spent all that money in improving the land and the outhouses of Penlon, he called up Silas and Nansi before him:

"Silas and Nansi," he said to them, "have I not been long-suffering with your filthy old ways?"

"Iss, indeed, little Abram," replied Nansi, "like the white little Jesus you are to us."

"You stink like an old sow, Nansi," said Abram.

Nansi whimpered: "Don't you be hard on me."

"Dear me now," Silas said, "do I not bear your old smell?"

"Ach y fi!" exclaimed Abram. "Move away. You stuff my nose."

Nansi moved back.

"Dear, dear," said Abram, "have I not prayed all the night then? The Big Man say you and Nansi must leave Penlon."

Nansi breathed: "Abram, little Abram bach, you won't send us off away?"

"You are a drag on the place," replied Abram. "Do not all speak about your mudlike ways, then? Every one got eleven pennies a pound for butter at Castellybryn on Friday; I got only ten pennies and three farthings. People said: 'Who will eat old Nansi's butter?'"

"Give him me a little bed alone in the barn loft, boy bach of God," said Silas.

"Why speak you so foolish?" said Abram. "Where am I to put the straw and the fowls? Little, blockhead bach, is your understanding! But I will not deal harshly with you. You two can live in Old Nanni's cottage. Very happy you'll be there. There's no rent to pay, and you, Silas, can mind my sheep on the moor."

"Man, man," cried Silas, "why should I leave Penlon? Did not my father give it to me?"

"Silas, indeed to goodness," said Abram, "for sure you are possessed. Religious Big Man, give you now me strength — the strength you gave the little Apostles — to cast out the Evil Spirit from old Silas."

He took in his hand his new carriage whip, and held it as he used to the thresher, and he brought the thong down upon Silas's back, and belly, and arms, and face.

Nansi made weepful sounds. She was very old, and she wept until she could weep no more.

When Silas's make-believe laughter was turned into yells of pain, Abram his son-in-law said:

"Get you up, now, Silas the sinner, and ask you the Big Man to forgive you your trespasses."

Silas and Nansi made ready to depart to the mud-walled, straw-thatched cottage in which the rats had bitten sores into old Nanni's face; before they set out, Abram brought to them Jos, Leisa's first-born child.

"Take you this brat of sin with you now, little people," he said, "for he is not of my bowels."

GREATER THAN LOVE

Esther knew the sun had risen because she could number the ripening cheeses arrayed on the floor against the wall. She threw back the shawl and sacks that covered her, and descending by the ladder into the kitchen, withdrew the bolt and opened the door.

"Goodness all! Late terrible am I," she said to the young man who entered. "Bring you the cows in a hurry, boy bach."

"Talk you like that, Esther, when the old animals are in the close."

Esther knelt on the hearth and lit the dried furze thereon.

"The buckets are in the milk-house," she went on. "Boy bach, hie you away off and make a start. Come I will as soon as I am ready."

The young man shuffled across the floor into the dairy. He came back with two buckets and a wooden tub, and he placed the tub on the ground and sat on its edge.

"This is the day of the seaside," he said.

Esther turned her face away from the smoke that ascended from the fire.

"Indeed, indeed, now, Sam bach!" she cried, "and you don't say so then!"

"Esther fach, vexful the move of your tongue. Say to me

whose cart is carting you?"

"Who speeched that I was going, Sam the son of Ginni?"

"Don't you be laughing, Esther. Tell me now whose cart is carting you."

"Go I would for sure into Morfa, but, dear me, no one will have me," said Esther.

"What for you cry mischief when there's no mischief to be?" said Sam.

Esther tore off pieces of peat and arranged them lightly on the furze.

"Nice place is Morfa," she observed.

"Girl fach, iss," Sam said. "Nice will be to go out in Twmmi's boat. Speak you that you will spend the day with me."

"How say Catrin! Sober serious! How will Catrin the daughter of Rachel speak if you don't go with her?"

"Mention you Catrin, Esther fach, what for?"

"Is there not loud speakings that you have courted Catrin in bed? Very full is her belly."

"Esther! Esther! Why you make me savage like an old rabbit? Why for play old pranks? Wench fach, others have been into Catrin. If I die, this is true. Do you believe me now?"

Esther plagued him, saying:

"Bring me small fairings home, Sam bach. Did I not give you a knife when I went to the Fair of the Month of April?"

Sam took out his knife, and sharpened the blade on the leather of his clog.

"Grateful was I for the nice knife," he said. "Did I not stick Old Shemmi's pig with it, Esther fach?"

"Well-well, then?"

"Look you, there's old murmuring that you were taken in mischief with the Schoolin' in Abram's hen loft," said Sam.

Esther rose to her feet and looked upon him. This is the manner of man she saw: a short, bent-shouldered, stunted youth; his face had never been shaved and was covered with tawny hair, and his eyes were sluggish.

Esther laughed.

"Boy bach, unfamiliar you are," she said.

"Mam did say," Sam proceeded, "that I ought not to wed a shiftless female who doesn't take Communion in Capel Sion."

"Your mother Old Ginni is right," said Esther. "Keep you on with Catrin. Ugly is Catrin with bad pimples in her face. But listen you, Sam; a large ladi I will be. I don't want louts like you."

The fire was under way; Esther rolled up to her waist her outer petticoat and she put on an apron.

"Why sit you there like a donkey?" she cried. "Away you and do the milking."

"Ester fach, come you to Morfa," Sam pleaded.

"For sure I'm coming to Morfa," Esther answered. "But not with you. Am I not going to find a love there?"

Then they went forth into the close to milk Old Shemmi's cows, and while they did so each chanted:

"There's a nice cow is Gwen!
  Milk she gives indeed!
More milk, little Gwen; more milk!
  A cow fach is Gwen," —

thereby coaxing the animals to give their full yield.

When the milk was separated Esther put on her Sabbath garments and drew her red hair tightly over her forehead, and she took her place in Shemmi's hay waggon. There were many in the waggon other than Esther and Sam, for the custom is that the farmer takes his servants and those who have helped him without payment in the hayfield freely on a set day to the Sea of Morfa.

Shemmi's waggon reached Morfa before the dew had lifted,

and towards the heat of the day (after they had eaten) the people of Manteg gathered together. One said: "Come you down to the brim now, and let us wash our little bodies." The men bathed nakedly: the women had brought spare petticoats with them, and these they wore when they were in the water.

Esther changed her behaviour when she got to Morfa, and she feigned herself above all who had come from Manteg, and while she sat alone in the shadow of a cliff there came to her Hws Morris, a young man who was in training to be a minister. Mishtir Morris was elegant: his clothes were black and he had a white collar around his neck and white cuffs at the ends of his sleeves, and on his feet he had brown shoes of canvas.

Hws Morris took off from his head his black hat, which was of straw, and said to Esther:

"Sure now, come you from Squire Pryce's household? You are his daughter indeed?"

"Stranger bach," answered Esther, "say you like that, what for?"

"A ladi you seem," said Hws Morris.

Esther was vain, and she did not perceive through the man's artifice.

"Indeed, indeed, then," said Hws Morris, "speak from where you are."

"Did you not say I was Squire Pryce's daughter?" said Esther.

"Ho, ho, old boy wise is Squire Pryce."

Esther turned her eyes upon the bathers. Catrin and another woman were knee-deep in the water; between them, their hands linked, Sam. She heard Bertha Daviss crying from the shore: "Don't you wet it, Sam bach."

Hws Morris placed the tips of his fingers into his ears.

"This," he mourned, "after two thousand years of religion. They need the little Gospel."

"Very respectable to be a preacher it is," said Esther.

"And to be a preacher's mistress," said Hws Morris. "Great is the work the Big Man has called me to do."

A murmuring came from the women on the beach: Sam was struggling in the water. Esther moved a little nearer the sea.

"Where was you going to, then?" asked Hws Morris. "You was not going to bathe with them?"

"Why for no?"

"See you how immodest they are. Girl fach, stay you here. If you need to wash your body, go you round to the backhead of the old stones and take off your clothes and bathe where no eyes will gaze on you."

The murmuring now sounded violent: Lloyd the Schoolin' was swimming towards Sam.

Esther passed beyond the stones, and in a cave she cast off her clothes and walked into the sea; and having cleansed herself, she dried her skin in the heat of the sun. When she got out from the cave, Hws Morris came up to her.

"Hungry you are," he said to her. "Return you into the cave and eat a little of this cake."

He led her far inside, so far they could not see anything that was outside. Hws Morris placed his arm over Esther's shoulders, and his white fingers moved lightly over her breast to her thigh. He stole her heart.

Esther heard a voice crying her name.

"Wench fach," said Hws Morris to her, "let none know of our business."

Sam shouted her name against the rocks and over the sea; he cried it in the ears of strange people and at the doors of strange houses. Towards dusk he said to the women who were waiting for Shemmi's hay waggon to start home: "Little females, why is Esther not here?"

Catrin jeered at him: "Filling her belly is Esther."

"But say you've seen Esther fach!" Sam cried.

"Twt, twt!" said Bertha Daviss. "What's the matter with the boy? Take him in your arms, Catrin, and take him to your bed."

"Speak you Esther is not drowned," Sam urged.

"Drowned!" Catrin repeated loudly. "Good if the bad concubine is."

"Evil is the wench," said Bertha Daviss. "Remember how she tried to snare Rhys Shop."

"Fond little women," Sam cried, "say you that Esther fach is not drowned."

"Sam, indeed to goodness," Bertha said to him, "trouble not your mind about a harlot."

"Now, dear me," answered Sam, "foolish is your speech, Bertha. How shall I come home without Esther?"

"There's Catrin, Sam bach. Owe you nothing to Catrin? Is she not in child by you?"

Old Shemmi's hay waggon came into the roadway, and Sam said to the man who drove the horse:

"Male bach nice, don't you begin before Esther comes, and she will be soon. Maybe she's sleeping."

"In the arms of a man," said Catrin.

Sam placed his hands around his mouth and shouted Esther's name.

The people entered the waggon: Sam remained in the road.

"Find you her, Sam bach!" Catrin cried. "Ask the Bad Spirit if he has seen her."

Old Shemmi's mare began the way home.

Sam hastened back to the beach: the tide was coming in, and he walked through the waters, shouting, moaning, and lamenting. At last he beheld Esther, and an awful wrath was kindled within him. As he had loved her, so he now hated her: he hated her even more than he had loved her. He had gone on the highway that ends in Llanon. At a little distance in front of him he saw her with a man, and he crept close to them and he heard their voices. He heard Esther saying:

"Don't you send me away now. Let me stay with you."

The man answered: "Shut your throat, you temptress. For why did you flaunt your body before my religious eyes?"

"Did you not make fair speeches to me?" said Esther.

"Terrible is your sin," said the man. "Turn away from me. Little Big Man bach, forgive me for eating of the wench's fruit."

Sam came up to them by stealth.

"Out of your head you must be, boy bach, to make sin with Esther," he said.

Hws Morris looked into Sam's face, and a horrid fear struck him, and he ran: and Sam opened his knife and running after him, caught him and killed him. He had difficulty in drawing away the blade, because it had entered into the man's skull. Then he returned to the place where Esther was, and her he killed also.

LAMENTATIONS

The Big Man despised Evan Rhiw, and said to the Respected Davydd Bern-Davydd, who then ruled from Capel Sion:

"Bern-Davydd, oppress Evan Rhiw. Go you off up and down the land now and say to the people: 'Lo, you animals in the image of the Big Man, God's blast is on the old male of Rhiw.'"

Bern-Davydd descended from the top of the moor and did according as he had been commanded; and his words got to the ears of Evan, who said: "Why must I be confused, dear me, because of that crow without sense, Bern-Davydd? Call you reasons to me."

Turning away from the man, the Judge of Sion answered by the mouth of Bertha Daviss (who was the tale bearer of the district): "Evan Rhiw, what are your works in Capel Sion? Did not the Big Man say, 'Bern bach, speak to me the sacrifices of Evan Rhiw for my Terrible Temple.' 'Little Big Man,' I answered, 'the least of my flock gives more than him.'" Then Bern-Davydd, by the mouth of Bertha, sang: "Evan Rhiw, swifter is the hand of the Lord than the water which turns Old Daniel's mill. Awful are the fingers that will grasp you by your rib trousers and throw you through the spouting flames into the Fiery Pool."

Evan did not regard this warning and stiffened his legs, because his substance consisted of fifty acres of land, a horse, three cows, and swine and hens: he was neither perfect nor upright, nor did he fear the men who sat in the high places in Capel Sion; and he revelled with loose, wild men in the inn which is kept by Mistress Shames.

Now the day the Big Man chastened him he drank much ale, and, unaware of what he was doing, he sinned against his daughter Matilda. In the morning he perceived what he had done, and was fearful lest his wife Hannah should revile him and speak aloud his wickedness. So, having laid a cunning snare for her, and finding that the woman did not know anything, he spoke to her harshly and without cause. This is what he said:

"Filthier you are than a cow."

"Evan, indeed to goodness," Hannah replied, "iobish you talk. Sober dear, do I not work to the bone?" With a knife she scraped through the refuse on her arm and displayed to him the thinness to which she referred. Then in her anger she spoke: "Slack you are, Evan Rhiw. Your little land you drink in the tavern of Mistress Shames. Are not the people mouthing your foolish ways on the tramping road and in Shop Rhys?"

Matilda entered the kitchen, and threw these words at him: "Dull and whorish you are, son of the Bad Spirit. Serious me, clean your smelly flesh in the pond."

Hannah interpreted the meaning of Matilda's words, and she reproached him bitterly.

But Evan answered none of the women. He went to the inn, and in his muddle he sorrowed: "Five over twenty years have I been wedded. When I took Hannah the servant of Bensha to my bed, rich was I. Did I not have six pairs of drawers, and six pairs of stockings, and six pairs of shirts of white linen? And three pairs of rib trousers? There's rib, people bach. Ninepence over half a crown a yard it cost in the Shop of the Bridge in Castellybryn. Not a shirt of linen do I possess this day. Wasteful has Hannah been with mine. Sad is my lot. Disorderly is the female, and Matilda says this and that about me to my discredit."

He brayed his woe also in the narrow Roman road which takes you past the Schoolhouse and in the path that cuts over Gorse Penparc into the field wherein stands Rhiw. At an early hour in the morning Matilda said to her mother: "Mam now, the cows fach are lowing to be milked," and receiving no answer she looked into Hannah's face and examined her body, and she saw that the woman was cold dead, whereupon she went out and into the stable, in the loft of which Evan slept, and cried up to him: "Father bach, do you stir yourself. Old mam has gone to wear a White Shirt."

While Sara Ann was clothing herself in mournful raiment Evan put on his clogs and went to the house of Lias the Carpenter, and to Lias he said: "The nice man, for why you don't know there is a desolate place in my heart this one minute? Come you with your little rule that shows the inches and measure the body of old Hannah for a coffin."

The second day that Hannah rested in the burial-ground of Capel Sion, Evan rubbed his face and hands with small gravel in the little water which runs at the foot of the close of Rhiw, and he drew a comb through his thinnish beard, and he walked to the house of Bern-Davydd.

"Respected and religious preacher," he said, "full of repentance am I, son of the little White Jesus."

"Happy you make me, Evan Rhiw," answered Bern-Davydd. "Grand will the angels sing, man, in the White Palace, when you take the communion. The wine, Evan, is it not the blood and the bread the flesh of the Big Man?"

"Discreet and wise ruler, let me make him a nice little offering."

"Religious proper, you are, Evan. Not to me, man, not to Mistress Bern-Davydd you make your sacrifices, but to the Big Man. I keep your gift in trust for Him. What shall I say is the name of the sacrifice, Evan bach?"

"This day the wench Sara Ann is churning, and is she not bringing him a pound of little butter?"

"Evan Rhiw, there is no sound of such a sacrifice in the Bible."

"And a tin pitcher full of buttermilk."

"Did Abram offer the three Strangers buttermilk, Evan?"

"And a big cabbage with a white heart."

"The Children of Israel, Evan bach, ate flesh."

"And a full wheelbarrow of potatoes."

"Tarry you awhile," said Bern-Davydd, "and I will commune with the Big Man." Presently he made utterance: "This is what the Great One of Capel Sion says: 'I will abate my oppression of Evan Rhiw if he makes a sacrifice of a pig.'"

Evan brought the pig; and he was admitted into Sion, and for two years he sinned not, and there was much pious joy in his way, and he prospered exceedingly. People said one to another: "Behold now, this man Evan is among the wisest in the Capel. And there's rich he is." Moreover he had given over feasting on the Devil's brew with loose, wild men, and his lips constantly moved in silent prayer, and he had respect for those who sat in the high places.

But as the man's possessions multiplied, his daughter Matilda got dull and became a cumbersome thing on him: and he charged the Big Man foolishly before the congregation of the Seiet. "Why, God bach," he said, "is your foot so heavy on me? Am I not religious? Ask you the Respected Davydd Bern-Davydd. Matilda is strange and amazed in her eyes, and she is set on mischief, and why brawls she loudly about me? Ach, indeed! Bad is this for your male son." For this God cursed his belongings: two horses sickened and perished, great rain fell upon his hay, which was ripe to be stacked; a cow destroyed her calf. The congregation was sore and murmured against him: "Pity now that our hay is rotting because of the bad sin of Evan Rhiw." A body of them wailed to Bern-Davydd.

"Speech him to the Great Harvester about this man Evan Rhiw," they said.

"Children bach," said Bern-Davydd, "run you about and about, and I will go to the top of the old moor and sing this lamentation to Him: 'Now then, why for you see our costly hay ruined? Is it a light thing that our precious animals starve throughout the hard days?'"

They looked at one another and marvelled at the familiarity between Bern-Davydd and the Big Man. "Sure," they said, "he is as important as God."

The third day the Judge of Sion commanded his flock to him, and he said to them: "Boys, boys, glad was the Big Man that I spoke to Him. Do you know what He said? 'Large thanks, Bern bach. Religious are you to remind me of the sin of Evan Rhiw. The man has a clean heart, and an adder in his house.' 'Big Man, don't you vex me,' I said. 'Whisper you me the name of the adder.' The Big Man said, 'Matilda. Evan may sin again, grievously, but I will restore him to Capel Sion, and I will bless him abundantly, for his freewill offerings to my Temple are generous.' Little boys, He went back to Heaven in a cloud, and the cloud was no bigger than the flat of this old hand."

The night of the Hiring Fair Evan drank in the inn, and the ale made him drunk, and he cried a ribald song; the men with whom he drank mocked him, and they carried him into the stable and laid him in a manger, and covered him with hay; and in the stall they put a horse, thinking the animal would eat Evan's hair and beard. But the Big Man watched over Evan, and the horse did not eat his beard.

"What shall we do," said the light men, "to humble him before the congregation?"

One said: "Let us strip the skin from the horse that perished, which is buried in the narrow field, and we will throw it over his head."

Thus they did, and Evan went home with the skin of the horse covering the back of him like a mantle.

His daughter Matilda saw him and was disturbed, and she kept out of his way until he slept. Then she issued forth from her hiding place, and said to herself: "Jesus bach, if the sons of men wear the habit of horses the daughters of God must go naked.' She cast from her body her clothes, and went down the Roman road and into the village. The people closed their doors on her, and for four days she wandered thereabouts nakedly. The men of the neighbourhood laid rabbit traps on the floor of the fields, and one trap caught the foot of Matilda, and she was delivered into Evan's hands. Having clothed her, he took a long rope, the length and thickness that is used to keep a load of hay intact, and one end of the rope he fastened round her right wrist and one end round the left wrist. In this wise he drove her before him, in the manner in which a colt is driven, to the madhouse of the three shires, which is in the town of Carmarthen, and the distance from Manteg to Carmarthen is twenty-four miles.

After that Evan did not sin any more; his belongings increased, and he had ten milching cows and five horses, and he hired a manservant and a maidservant, and he rented twenty-five acres of land over and beyond the land that was his, and his house remained religious as long as he lived.

THE BLAST OF GOD

Owen Tygwyn — Tygwyn is the zinc-roofed house that is in a group of trees at the back of Capel Sion — was ploughing when his wife Shan came to the break in the hedge, crying:

"For what you think, little man? Dai is hanging in the cowhouse. Come you now and see to him."

Owen ended the furrow and unharnessed the horse, which he led into the stable and fed with hay. Then he unravelled the knot in the rope which had choked the breath of his son Dai. When he was finished and Dai was laid on the floor of the cowhouse, Shan said to him:

"Eat you your middle-of-the-day morsel now, before you go back to the old plough."

Having eaten to his liking of the beaten potatoes and buttermilk, Owen resumed his labour, and while he was labouring he rehearsed a prayer he would make for a male child, and that prayer he said to the Big Husband at the far end of the light. His petition reached the ears of God, and after twenty months it was answered: the cry of the infant woke him, and he got out of bed and lit a tallow candle, and read his Bible, because he was very glad. With the rising of the sun he brought his three cows into the close.

"Lissi Mari," he said to his daughter, who slept at the foot of the bed, "get you up now, wench fach, and milk the creatures, for things are so-so with Shan. Are not their old udders bursting?"

The child was named Samuel, and in Capel Sion on the Sabbath Owen glorified the Big Man.

But his words were not pleasing to Joshua Lancoch, who corrected him, saying:

"An old veil females wear must divide you from the face of the Big Man. Indeed, like lead is my heart for you. Overvain you are to expect too much from your brat. He is not of the Lord's giving."

"Sober, Joshua," said Owen, "speak you out, dear me, there's a wise little man."

"Well-well, now, ill is my stomach to make speech, but Shan is a miscarrying woman, and a miscarrying woman is dung in the nose of the Man of Terror. Two she miscarried before Dai, Owen bach, and Dai hanged himself to the Fiery Pool in the cowhouse. Ach y fi! Do you be humble, and tempt you the Big Man not overmuch. He is quick to anger."

Because of this chiding Owen entreated the Lord continually, and he also made sacrifices unto Capel Sion: his possessions got small and he whipped his spirit into humility and subjection, for is it not written that the meek shall inherit the Kingdom? He sold live stock to pay his rent, and this stock he was never able to replace. After the birth of Samuel Shan miscarried two children, and the price of two pigs provided them with coffins and graves.

In his bitterness Owen turned to his wife and said: "Pity the Big Man has made you such a spoilful curse."

Shan spread her hands over her wasteful breasts, and moaned:

"Make you not that speech, little Owen. Have you not Samuel? Did not the Great Husband send him in answer to your prayer?"

"Right true, Shan. Now indeed, pious the boy bach is."

"Iss-iss. Does he not tongue prayers like a preacher? And his learning is more than the old Schoolin's."

"Why you speak stupid for, woman? That old blockhead of a Schoolin' knows nothing."

"Grand will be if we send him to the School of Grammar in Castellybryn."

"Iss, dear me."

"Holy joy will be to listen to him preach the Word."

"Sam bach will make everyone weep with his eloquence."

Owen called his son to him.

"Stand you on an old chair," he said to him, "and say out a small hymn and make a bit of prayer."

When the lad finished, Owen said:

"Well done, little boy bach clever. Did I not think I was in Capel Sion?"

"Pretty his speech," exclaimed Shan. "Heard you how he sang, 'Be with Thy nice servant bach in the Temple of Sion, prosper his work among the sinful congregation'?"

Samuel passed the seventh standard in the School of Lloyd, whereat Owen, asked in the Seiet to bear testimony, spoke these words:

"Do you be glad with me that the Big Man has inspired my son Samuel to noise abroad His Word. Has not the Lord been good to me then? You all know that Shan is a miscarrying woman. Yet lo, He blesses her iniquity. Mouth you this miracle throughout all the land."

In due season he went to Castellybryn and said to the Chief Teacher of the School of Grammar:

"Mishtir bach, make you room for my son Samuel, the child the Big Husband sent in answer to my groanings."

The day of the Harvest Fair he journeyed there again, and he drove before him a cow in calf, and one part of the money he got for the animal he gave to the Chief Teacher, and with the other part he caused to be made for Samuel a preacher's coat, which is of shiny black material.

Owen and Shan bent their backs and tilled and turned the soil, but they reaped less than they sowed. Lissi Mari became a servant-maid on Abel's farm (which is on the sea side of the moor). Before the term of her hire was over she returned to her father's house.

"Lissi Mari is carrying her cross," Shan mourned.

"We will keep this a secret from my son," said Owen. "Very holy must his thoughts be stored."

Samuel entered College Carmarthen, and Owen sold two sheep so that his son might have clothes that would be for glory and holiness.

"That's fair, little man," said Shan. "He must be kept presentable," and every Friday she killed a fattened hen and had it sent to the house where he lodged.

For all that Owen and Shan did, Samuel was grateful and he said: "In me they will find their stronghold"; and in the call of Capel Bethel, in Morfa, he distinguished the voice of God.

And Owen said to his wife Shan:

"The Great Father is repenting of His doings against you, Shan fach."

"Little man, iss. Iss, little man," she answered gladly. "Joyful am I to see the boy in the pulpit."

As their souls rejoiced, the weariness which follows heavy toil made their bones stiff. Shan was flat and unlovely, and of the colour of earth. Except on the Sabbath she covered her bosom with many shawls and a discarded waistcoat, and in the wrinkles of her face there was much dirt.

There was a day when Samuel came to Tygwyn and looked upon the burdens of his father and mother, and he said to them:

"People bach, leave Tygwyn and go you and abide in the cottage against the back of Shop Rhys. Take you Lissi Mari's baby."

"Foolish is your speech," said Shan. "How shall we fend without a little cow and a little pig?"

"Am I not of your flesh?" asked Samuel.

"Gift of the Big Father, good are you," and the woman shivered in her happiness, and Owen and Shan lifted their feet and took all that was in the house and went to abide in the place appointed by Samuel.

Three years passed. Lissi Mari was out in the world. Owen was a power in Capel Sion, for the brand was lifted from the face of Shan.

Then a horrible thing happened: Samuel wrought folly in Capel Bethel, in Morfa, and the sound of it reached the high places of all the Capels.

Hugh Morgan, a deacon in Bethel, stopped his pony in front of Shop Rhys.

"Show him me the abode of Owen the Father of Samuel the minister of Bethel," he said to Rhys.

Rhys asked: "Explain him to me his little errand now, dear stranger."

"Little man who sells things in a shop, why for will he plead? Take him me now hasty to the place."

"Tell him me then at once quickly," said Rhys.

"Has he not heard of this infamy? Man, man, Samuel the son of Satan has hanged his clay."

"Solemn! Solemn!"

"Was not the nanny-goat the father of Esther's child? Esther the daughter of Shon of the Boats?"

"Speak he like that now?"

"Was there not a meeting of First Men the last night, and did I not accuse him? 'You put her big,' I speeched."

"Talk in that manner then?" said Rhys of the Shop. "What glory has ever come from a miscarrying woman?"

Rhys Shop and Hugh Morgan went into the house of Owen and Shan.

"For shame, man of the bad," said Rhys. "And you too, Shan, the serpent in the Great One's Temple. An old abomination you are then! There was Dai, and the dead, though not born. And now Samuel."

"Dear little Rhys, harsh are your words," said Owen.

Hugh Morgan stood on the threshold. "Dear me, man," he said to Rhys, "there's a talker he is for sure! Am I not the messenger?" Then he turned to Owen and Shan and spoke to them wrathfully: "Is not Samuel the father of Esther's child? And has he not hanged himself?"

"Shame on you, sinners," said Rhys.

"Fetch you Satan's carcase away this day," said Hugh Morgan. "The smelly clay is lying in my barn. Fetch you the unholy object."

Owen hired a cart and horse and he placed three sacks and a little straw on the floor of the cart; and Shan said to him: "Hide you this little patchwork quilt under the sacks and straw, for fear men's eyes will see it and jeer at you."

Before departing, Owen said:

"Go you and dig a grave and have it ready that we can bury your son this night. Leave space between Dai's and his for my coffin. When the Big Trumpet tones I will rise early and make excuses to the Angel not to be too hard on your sons as they were born of a miscarrying woman."

BIBLIOGRAPHY

My People, published by Andrew Melrose in early November 1915, passed through six editions within four years. The strategy behind the first physical presentation of the text is discussed by John Harris, 'Publishing *My People*: the book as expressive object', *New Welsh Review* I (1988), 23-30; Harris also considers author-publisher relationships in 'From his presbyterian pinnacle: Caradoc Evans and Andrew Melrose', *Planet* 90 (1991-1992), 31-37.

For contemporary English reaction see *Bookman,* Christmas 1915 (Edwin Pugh), *English Review,* Dec 1915 (Norman Douglas), *Evening News,* 12 Nov 1915 (Arthur Machen), *New Witness,* 16 Mar 1916, *Reynolds's Weekly Newspaper,* 2 Jan 1916 (Alan Stephens), *Sphere,* 11 Dec 1915 (Clement Shorter), *Times Literary Supplement,* 4 Nov 1915, and *Westminster Gazette,* 27 Nov 1915.

Welsh reaction can be sampled in *Cambria Daily Leader,* 29 Oct 1915, *Carmarthen Journal,* 17 Dec 1915, *Labour Voice/Llais Llafur,* 6 Nov 1915 (W.H. Stevenson), *Western Mail,* 13 Nov 1915, and *Welsh Outlook,* 3 Mar 1916 (Ivor John). The *Western Mail*'s battle with Caradoc is examined by Trevor Williams, 'The birth of a reputation: early Welsh reaction to the work of Caradoc Evans', *Anglo-Welsh Review* 19, 44 (1971), 147-171, which quotes extensively from reviews and correspondence occasioned by Evans's first three books.

Specific comment on *My People* is to be found in Trevor Williams, Caradoc Evans (1970), a useful introductory guide, and in A.J. Smith and W.H. Mason, *Short Story Study: A Critical Anthology* (1961), illuminating on 'Be This Her Memorial'. More recent critical writing includes two articles by Mary Jones, 'The satire of Caradoc Evans', *Anglo-Welsh Review* 72 (1982), 58-65, and 'A changing myth: the projection of the Welsh in the short stories of Caradoc Evans', *Anglo-Welsh Review* 81 (1985), 90-99; John Barnie, 'Caradoc Evans: the impious artist', *Planet* 53 (1985), 64-69; John Davies and John Harris, 'Caradoc Evans and the forcers of conscience: a reading of "A Father in Sion"', *Anglo-Welsh Review* 81 (1985), 79-89; M. Wynn Thomas, '*My People* and the revenge of the novel', *New Welsh Review* 1 (1988), 17-22; Regina Weingartner, 'The fight against sentimentalism; Caradoc Evans and George Douglas Brown', *Planet* 75 (1989), 86-92; W.J. Rees, 'Inequalities: Caradoc Evans and D.J. Williams', *Planet* 81 (1990), 69-80; Simon Baker, 'Caradoc Evans's "A Father in Sion" and contemporary critical theory', *New Welsh Review* 11 (1991), 46-50; and D.Z. Phillips, 'Distorting truth (Caradoc Evans)', in his *From Fantasy to Faith: the Philosophy of Religion and Twentieth Century Literature* (1991), pp. 84-94.

Evan's place in Anglo-Welsh literature is considered by Glyn Jones, *The Dragon Has Two Tongues* (1968), and by Gwyn Jones, *The First Forty Years: Some Notes on Anglo-Welsh Literature* (1957). Gwyn Jones has championed Evans at every turn, never more persuasively than in 'Caradoc Evans', *Welsh Review* 4, 1 (Mar 1945), 74-78, and 'Let My People Go', *TLS*, 9 Jan 1969, 33-34 (jointly the basis of 'A mighty man in Sion: Caradoc Evans, 1878-1945', in Gwyn Jones, *Background to Dylan Thomas and Other Explorations,* 1992). A third distinguished Welsh short-story writer, Leslie Norris, assesses Caradoc Evans in a review of the reprinted *My People, Powis Review* 23 (1989) 71-72.

Turning to biographical studies, the extended introduction to *Fury Never Leaves Us: A Miscellany of Caradoc Evans*, ed. John Harris (1985), surveys the entire career; more specifically, Harris considers the childhood in '"Dai Lanlas": the schoolboy at Rhydlewis', *Ceredigion: Journal of the Ceredigion Antiquarian Society* 10, 4 (1987), 431-449, and his work as journalist at the time of *My People*, in 'Caradoc Evans as editor of *Ideas*', *Planet* 53 (1985), 52-63. David Jenkins, 'Community and kin: Caradoc Evans "at home"' *Anglo-Welsh Review* 24, 53 (1974), 43-57, treats of immediate family and community, while George Green, in his introduction to Caradoc Evans, *The Earth Gives All And Takes All* (1946), writes convincingly from a position of close friendship.

Oliver Sandys, *Caradoc Evans* (1946) is a biography by the author's second wife, Marguerite (herself a romantic novelist, writing also under the name of Countess Barcynska). A blend of fact and speculation, and lacking in documentation, the book should be approached cautiously, though it does suggest the uncomfortable truths of Evan's post-Fleet Street years.

For background see David Jenkins, *The Agricultural Community in South West Wales at the Turn of the Twentieth Century* (1971). Based on the parish of Troedyraur (which includes Rhydlewis) this work is of particular interest to students of Caradoc Evans.

Addendum

The most complete bibliography of Caradoc Evans is that in John Harris, *A Bibliographical Guide to Twenty-Four Modern Anglo-Welsh Authors* (1994), pp. 69-70. Subsequent biographical and critical essays include: John Harris, 'The Devil in Eden: Caradoc Evans and his Wales', *New Welsh Review* 19 (1992-93), 10-18, 'Caradoc Evans: my people right or wrong', *Transactions of the Honourable Society of Cymmrodorion* 1995, new series 2 (1996), 141-155, Chris Hopkins, 'James Joyce is an Irish edition of Mr Caradoc Evans: two Celtic naturalists', *Irish Studies Review* 12 (1995), 23-26, Barbara Prys-Williams, 'Fury never left him: the psychology of Caradoc Evans', *New Welsh Review* 31 (1995-96), 60-62, Gerwyn Williams, 'Gwerin dau Garadog', in *Diffinio dwy lenyddiaeth Cymry,* ed. M. Wynn Thomas (1995), pp. 42-79, on Caradoc Evans and Caradog Prichard.

ACKNOWLEDGEMENTS

I am indebted to the following for permission to reproduce copyright material: Nicholas Sandys (literary executor), the Librarian, National Library of Wales (photographs from the John Thomas collection for the cover and plates 4 and 5), Mrs Lil Powell (page 7 photograph). Plates 2 and 3 are taken from postcards kindly supplied by Mr David Powell. I should also like to thank the late Professor Gwyn Jones for allowing me to consult and quote from material in the privately-owned Caradoc Evans Papers.

SEREN CLASSICS

Well chosen words

Seren is an independent publisher with a wide-ranging list which includes poetry, fiction, biography, art, translation, criticism and history. Many of our authors have been on longlists and shortlists – and have won – major literary prizes. among them the Costa Award, the Man Booker, the Desmond Elliott Prize, the Ondaatje Prize, the Writers' Guild Award, the Forward Prize and the T.S. Eliot Prize.

At the heart of our list is a good story told well or an idea or history presented interestingly or provocatively. We're international in authorship and readership though our roots are here in Wales (Seren means 'star' in Welsh), where we prove that writers from a small country with an intricate culture have a worldwide relevance.

Our aim is to publish work of the highest literary and artistic merit that also succeeds commercially in a competitive, fast-changing environment. You can help us achieve this goal by reading more of our books – available from all good bookshops and increasingly as e-books. You can also buy them at a 20% discount from our website, and get updates about forthcoming titles, readings, launches and other news about Seren and the authors we publish.

www.serenbooks.com